Brides for Brothers

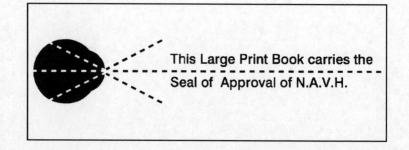

This Large Print Book carries the
Seal of Approval of N.A.V.H.

MIDNIGHT SONS, BOOK 1

BRIDES FOR BROTHERS

DEBBIE MACOMBER

THORNDIKE PRESS

A part of Gale, Cengage Learning

Farmington Hills, Mich • San Francisco • New York • Waterville, Maine
Meriden, Conn • Mason, Ohio • Chicago

GALE
CENGAGE Learning

LIBRARY OF CONGRESS CATALOGING-IN-PUBLICATION DATA

Macomber, Debbie.
  Brides for brothers / by Debbie Macomber. — Large print edition.
    pages ; cm. — (Midnight sons ; #1) (Thorndike Press large print romance)
  ISBN 978-1-4104-6997-7 (hardcover) — ISBN 1-4104-6997-2 (hardcover)
  1. Brothers—Fiction. 2. Brides—Fiction. 3. Alaska—Fiction. 4. Large type books. I. Title.
PS3563.A2364B754 2014
813'.54—dc23   2014008398

Published in 2014 by arrangement with Harlequin Books S.A.

Printed in the United States of America
1 2 3 4 5 6 7 18 17 16 15 14

For Don and Mary Ann Adler
Don is my oldest cousin and
Mary Ann one of my
dearest friends and a fellow
cameo collector

Dear Friends,
Welcome to Hard Luck, Alaska, a small community near the Arctic Circle. The town has a rich and interesting history that I hope you'll enjoy. These books revolve around the three O'Halloran brothers — Sawyer, Charles and Christian — who own a flight service. The problem is, they keep losing their best pilots, until the brothers decide that the way to keep the men is to recruit women to their town. That's when the fun begins.

My husband worked on the Arctic pipeline back in the mid-1980s and came to love Alaska. Creating this series was the perfect opportunity for me to explore it for myself. Our

7

research trip in the summer of 1994 proved to be one of the most rewarding and enjoyable experiences of my writing career. I fell hopelessly in love with Alaska, the sheer magnificence of the landscape, the vastness and beauty, the friendliness of the small towns. Even now, all these years later, I have warm memories of our time there. Wayne and I flew with bush pilots, trekked across the tundra and talked with anyone who was willing to tell us about their lives.

The Midnight Sons series holds a special place in my heart. It was the prelude to the Heart of Texas series, the Dakota books and eventually led to the Cedar Cove series. (Keep in mind that the Hard Luck stories were written in the mid-nineties, before cell phones, DVDs and the Internet became part of our everyday lives.)

Now I invite you to sit back and allow me to introduce you to some proud, stubborn, wonderful men — Alaska men — and show you what happens when they meet their matches. Women from the "lower forty-eight." Women a lot like you and me.

Debbie Macomber

P.S. By the way, I love hearing from readers. You can reach me at www .debbiemacomber.com or by mail at P.O. Box 1458, Port Orchard, Washington 98366.

THE HISTORY OF
HARD LUCK, ALASKA

Hard Luck, situated fifty miles north of the Arctic Circle, near the Brooks Range, was founded by Adam O'Halloran and his wife, Anna, in 1931. Adam came to Alaska to make his fortune, but never found the gold strike he sought. Nevertheless, the O'Hallorans and their two young sons, Charles and David, stayed on — in part because of a tragedy that befell the family a few years later.

Other prospectors and adventurers began to move to Hard Luck, some of them bringing wives and children. The town became a stopping-off place for mail, equipment and supplies. The Harmon family arrived in 1938 to open a dry goods store, and the Fletchers came soon after that.

When World War II began, Hard Luck's population was fifty or sixty people all told. Some of the young men, including the O'Halloran sons, joined the armed services; Charles left for Europe in 1942, David in 1944 at the age of eighteen. Charles died during the fighting. Only David came home — with a young English war bride, Ellen Sawyer, despite the fact that he'd become engaged to Catherine Harmon shortly before going overseas. (Catherine married Willie Fletcher after David's return.)

After the war, David qualified as a bush pilot. He then built some small cabins to attract the sport fishermen and hunters who were starting to come to Alaska; he also worked as a guide. Eventually he built a lodge to replace the cabins — a lodge that was later damaged by fire.

David and Ellen had three sons, born fairly late in their marriage — Charles (named after David's brother) was born in 1960, Sawyer in 1963 and Christian in 1965.

Hard Luck had been growing slowly all this time and by 1970 it was home to just over a hundred people. These were the years of the oil boom, when the school and community center were built by the state. After Vietnam, ex-serviceman Ben Hamilton joined the community and opened the Hard Luck Café, which became the social focus for the town.

In the late 1980s the three O'Halloran brothers formed a partnership, creating Midnight Sons, a bush-pilot operation. They were awarded the mail contract, and they also deliver fuel and other necessities to the interior. In addition, they serve as a small commuter airline, flying passengers to and from Fairbanks and within the northern Arctic.

In 1995, at the time these stories start, there were approximately 150 people living in Hard Luck — the majority of them male. . . .

Now, almost fifteen years later, join the people here in looking back at their history — particularly the changes that occurred when Midnight Sons invited women to town. Women who transformed Hard Luck, Alaska, forever!

PROLOGUE

June 1995

"What you really need are *women.*"

Sawyer O'Halloran made a show of choking on his coffee. "Women! We've got enough problems!"

Ben Hamilton — the Hard Luck Café's owner, cook and just about everything else — set the coffeepot on the counter. "Didn't you just tell me Phil Duncan's decided to move back to Fairbanks?"

Phil was the best pilot Sawyer had. He wasn't the first one Midnight Sons had lost to the big city, either. Every time a pilot resigned, it was a setback for the Arctic flight service.

"Yes, but Phil's not leaving because of a woman," Sawyer said.

"Sure he is," Duke Porter piped up. Still clutching his mug, he slipped onto the stool next to Sawyer. "Phil quit because he couldn't see his girlfriend as much as he wanted. He might've given you some phony excuse when he handed in his notice, but you know as well as I do why he quit."

"Joe and Harlan left because of women, too. Because they couldn't meet any, not if they were living here!" It was Ben again. The ex-Navy "stew burner" — as the

O'Halloran brothers called him —
obviously had strong views on the
subject. Sawyer often shared his
opinions, but not this time. He had
half a mind to suggest Ben keep his
nose out of this, but that wouldn't
be fair.

One of the problems with living
in a small town, especially if you'd
grown up there, was that you knew
everyone, Sawyer reflected. And
everyone knew you — *and* your
business.

He might as well set up the Midnight Sons office right here in the
middle of the café. His pilots rou-
tinely ate breakfast at Ben's, and
the cook was as familiar with the
air charter's troubles as the brothers were themselves.

Christian, the youngest O'Halloran, held his mug with both hands. "All right, if you won't say it, I will," he began, looking pointedly at Sawyer. "Ben's right. Bringing a few women to Hard Luck would keep the crew happy."

Sawyer didn't really disagree with him. "We've got a new schoolteacher coming. A woman." As a member of the school board, Sawyer had read over Bethany Ross's application and been impressed with her qualifications, but he wasn't sure the state should have hired her. She'd been born and raised in California. He still hadn't figured out why she'd applied for a teaching position north of the Arctic Circle.

"I just hope this teacher isn't like the last one," John Henderson grumbled. "I flew her in, remember? I was as polite as could be, circled the area a bit, showed her the sights from the air, talked up the town. The woman wouldn't even get off the plane."

"I'd still like to know what you said to her," Christian muttered.

"I didn't say anything," John insisted. "I mean, besides what I told you." He squinted at Sawyer. "The new teacher's not coming until August, is she?"

"August," Ben repeated. "*One* woman." He readjusted the stained white apron around his thick waist. "I can see it now."

"See what?" Fool that he was,

Sawyer had to ask. It went without saying that Ben would be more than happy to tell him.

"One woman will cause more problems than she'll solve," Ben said in a portentous voice. "Think about it, Sawyer."

Sawyer didn't want to think about it. All this talk of bringing in women made him uncomfortable.

"One thing's for sure, we're not going to let John fly her in this time," Ralph said scornfully. "I got first dibs."

He was answered by a loud chorus of "Like hell!" and "No way!"

"Don't squabble!" Sawyer shouted.

Ben chuckled and slid a plate of sourdough hotcakes onto the counter toward Ralph.

"See what I mean?" the cook said under his breath. "Your men are already fighting over the new teacher, and she isn't even arriving for months."

Ralph lit into the hotcakes as if he hadn't eaten in a week. Mouth full, he mumbled something about lonely bachelors.

"All right, all right," Sawyer conceded. "Bringing a few women to Hard Luck might be a good idea, but how do you suggest we persuade them to move up here?"

"I guess we could advertise," Christian said thoughtfully, then brightened. "Sure, we'll advertise. It's a good idea. I don't know why we didn't think of it sooner."

"Advertise?" Sawyer glared at his brother. "What do you mean, *advertise*?"

"Well, we could put an ad in one of those glossy magazines women like to buy. You know, the kind with *lifestyle* articles." He said the word almost reverently. "What I heard, it's gotten to be the thing to place an ad about lonely men in Alaska seeking companionship."

"A friend of a friend sent his picture to one of 'em," Ralph said excitedly, "and before he knew it, he had a sackful of letters. All from women eager to meet him."

"I want you to know right now I'm not taking off my shirt and posing for any damn picture," Duke Porter said in an emphatic voice.

24

"Getting your photograph in one of those magazines isn't as easy as it sounds," Ralph warned after swallowing a huge bite. He shrugged. "Not that I've tried or anything."

"Things are rarely as good as they sound," Sawyer pointed out reasonably, pleased that at least one of his employees was thinking clearly.

"Those women aren't looking for pen pals, you know," John said. "They're after husbands, and they aren't the type who can be picky, either, if you catch my drift."

"So? You guys aren't exactly centerfold material yourselves," Ben was quick to remind them. He pushed up the sleeves of his shirt and planted both hands on the counter.

"As far as I can see," Sawyer said, "we don't have anything to offer women. It's not like our good looks would induce them to move here, now is it?"

John's face fell with disappointment. "You're probably right."

"What would work, then?" Christian asked. "We need to think positive, or we're going to end up spending our lives alone."

"I don't have any complaints about *my* life," Sawyer told his brother. Christian's enthusiasm for this crazy idea surprised him. Sawyer was willing to go along with it, but he didn't have much faith in its success. For one thing, he wasn't convinced there'd be any takers.

And if there were, the presence of these women might create a whole new set of problems.

"You've got to remember women aren't that different from men," Christian was saying, sounding like a TV talk-show expert.

The others stared at him, and Christian laughed. "You know what I mean. You guys came up to Hard Luck, didn't you? Even though we're fifty miles north of the Arctic Circle."

"Sure," Duke answered. "But the wages are the best around, and the living conditions aren't bad."

"Wages," Christian said, removing a pen from the pocket of his plaid shirt. He made a note on his paper napkin.

"You aren't thinking about *paying* women to move to Hard Luck, are you?" Sawyer would fight that idea tooth and nail. He'd be darned if he'd see his hard-earned cash wasted on such foolishness.

"We could offer women jobs, couldn't we?" Christian asked. He glanced around to gather support from the other pilots.

"Doing what?" Sawyer demanded.

"Well . . ." Frowning, his brother gnawed on the end of his pen. "You've been saying for a long time that we need to get the office organized. How about hiring a secretary? You and I have enough to do dealing with everything else. It's a mess, and we can't seem to get ahead."

Sawyer resisted the urge to suggest a correspondence course in time management. "All right," he said grudgingly.

The other pilots looked up from their breakfasts. They were beginning to take notice.

"What about all those books your mother left behind after she married Frank?" Ben asked. "She donated them so Hard Luck could have a library."

Sawyer gritted his teeth. "A volunteer library."

"But someone's got to organize it," Christian said. "I've tried now and then, but whenever I start to get things straightened out, I'm overwhelmed. There must be a thousand books there."

Sawyer couldn't really object, since, unlike Christian, he'd never made any effort to put his mother's collection in order.

"That was very generous of your mother, giving the town her books," Ralph said. "But it's a shame we can't find what we want or check it out if we do."

"It seems to me," Christian said, smiling broadly, "that we could afford to pay someone to set up the library and run it for a year or so. Don't you agree?"

Sawyer shrugged. "If Charles does." But they both knew their oldest brother would endorse the idea. He'd been wanting to get the library going for quite a while.

"I heard Pearl say she was thinking of moving to Nenana to live with her daughter," Ben told the gathering. "In that case, the town's going to need someone with medical experience for the health clinic."

A number of heads nodded. Sawyer suspected now was not the time to remind everyone that Pearl regularly mentioned moving in with her daughter. Generally the sixty-year-old woman came up with that idea in the darkest part of winter, when there were only a couple of hours of daylight and spirits were low.

"I know what you're thinking," Ben said, turning to Sawyer. "But did it ever occur to you that Pearl actually *would* leave if someone was here to take over for her?"

No, Sawyer hadn't. Pearl had lived in Hard Luck for as long as he could remember. She'd been a friend of his mother's when Ellen lived in Hard Luck, and a peace-maker in the small community. Over the years Sawyer had frequently had opportunity to be grateful to Pearl. If she did decide to move, he'd miss her.

"We can ask her if she's serious about wanting to retire," Sawyer agreed, despite his reluctance. "But I won't have Pearl thinking we don't want her."

"I'll talk to her myself," Christian promised.

"I could use a bit of help around here," Ben said. "I've been feeling my age of late."

"You mean feeling your oats, don't you?" John teased.

Ben grinned. "Go ahead and add a part-time cook and waitress to your list."

There were smiles all around. Sawyer hated to be the one to put a damper on all these plans, but someone had to open their eyes to a few truths. "Has anyone figured out where these women are going to live?"

It was almost comical to see the smiles fall in unison, as if they were marionettes and a puppetmaster was working their mouths. Still, Sawyer had to admit he was beginning to warm to the idea of recruiting women. Hard Luck could do with a few new faces and he wouldn't object if those faces happened to be young, female and pretty. Not that *he* was the marrying kind. No, sirree. Not Sawyer O'Halloran. Not after what he'd seen with his parents. Their unhappiness had taught him early and taught him well that marriage meant misery. Although, in his opinion, Catherine Fletcher bore a lot of the blame. . . .

He shook his head. Marriage was definitely out, and he suspected his two brothers felt the same way. They must. Neither of them seemed inclined toward marriage, either.

He returned his attention to the dilemma at hand. No one appeared to have any answers to his question about where these women would live, and Sawyer felt obligated to point out the less-than-favorable aspects of their plan. The more he considered it, the more certain he became that this idea was impossible. Attractive, perhaps — especially in a moment of weakness — but impossible.

"It wouldn't have worked, anyway," he said.

"Why not?" his brother asked.

"Women are never satisfied with the status quo. They'd move to Hard Luck and immediately want to change things." Sawyer had seen it before. "Well, *I* don't want things changed. We have it good here."

"Yeah," Ralph agreed, but without much enthusiasm.

"Before we knew it," Sawyer continued, "the ladies would have rings on their fingers and rings through our noses, and they'd be leading us around like . . . like sheep. Worse, they'd convince us that's the way we want it."

"Nope. Not going to happen to me," John vowed. "Unless . . ."

Not giving him a chance to weaken, Sawyer went on. "We'd be making runs into Fairbanks for low-fat ice cream because one or other of them has a craving for chocolate without the calories." Sawyer could picture it now. "They'd want us to watch our language and turn the TV off during dinner and shave every day . . . and . . ."

"You're right," Duke said with conviction. "A woman would probably want me to shave off my beard."

The men grimaced as if they could already feel the razor.

Women in Hard Luck would have his pilots wrapped around their little fingers within a week, Sawyer thought. And after that, his men wouldn't be worth a damn.

Christian hadn't spoken for several minutes. Now he slowly rubbed his hand along his jaw. "What about the cabins?"

"The old hunting cabins your father built on the outskirts of town?" Ralph asked.

Sawyer and Christian exchanged a look. "Those are the ones," Christian said. "Dad built them back in the fifties before the lodge was completed — you know, the lodge that burned down? Folks would fly in for hunting and fishing and he'd put them up there. They're simple, one medium-size room without any conveniences."

"No one's lived in those cabins for years," Sawyer reminded his brother.

"But they're solid, and other than a little dirt there's nothing wrong with them. Someone could live there. Easily." Christian's voice rose as he grew excited about the idea. "With a little soap and water and a few minor repairs, they'd be livable in nothing flat."

Sawyer couldn't believe what he

was hearing. A city gal would take one look at those cabins and leave on the next flight out. "But there isn't any running water or electricity."

"No," Christian agreed, "not yet."

Now Sawyer understood, and he didn't like it. "I'm not putting any money into fixing up those run-down shacks." Charles would have a fit if he let Christian talk him into doing anything so stupid.

"Those old cabins aren't worth much, are they?" Christian asked.

Sawyer hesitated. He recognized his brother's tone. Christian had something up his sleeve.

"No," Sawyer admitted cautiously.

"Then it wouldn't hurt to give the

cabins away."

"Give them away?" Sawyer echoed. It stood to reason that no one would *pay* for them. Who'd want them anyway, even if they were free?

"We're going to need something to induce women to move to Hard Luck," Christian said. "We aren't offering them marriage."

"Damn right we're not." John gulped down a slug of coffee and wiped his mouth with the back of his hand.

"Companionship is all I'm interested in," another of the pilots added. "Female companionship."

"We don't want to mislead anyone into thinking this is about marriage."

"Exactly."

Sawyer looked around the room at his pilots. "Marriage is what practically all women are after," he said with more certainty than he actually felt.

"There's plenty of jobs in the lower forty-eight," Christian said in a perfectly reasonable tone. This was always where Sawyer ran into trouble with his younger brother. Christian could propose the most ridiculous idea in the most logical way. "True?"

"True," Sawyer agreed warily.

"So, like I said before, we've got to offer these women some incentive to live and work in Hard Luck."

"You want to give them the cabins?" Sawyer scratched his head.

"As an *incentive*?"

"Sure. Then if they want to bring in electricity and running water they can do it with their own money."

Sawyer checked around to see what the others were thinking. He couldn't find a dissenting look among them. Not on Ben's face and certainly not on any of the others. He should've known Christian's idea would take root in the fertile minds of his women-starved men.

"We'd clean up the cabins a bit first," Christian said as though this was the least they could do.

"We found a bear in one of them last year," Sawyer reminded his brother.

"That bear didn't mean any harm," Ralph said confidently. "He was just having a look around, is all. I doubt he'll be back after the shot of pepper spray Mitch gave him."

Sawyer just shook his head, bemused.

"But it might not be smart to mention the bear to any of the women," Ben was quick to add. "Women are funny about wild critters."

"Yeah," John said in hushed tones, "take my word for it — don't say anything about the wildlife."

"Say anything?" Sawyer asked. The men made it sound like he was going to personally interview each applicant.

"To the women when you talk to them," Ralph explained with exaggerated patience.

"I'm going to be talking to these women?"

"Why, sure," Duke said, as if that had been understood from the beginning. "You'll have to interview them, you or Christian. Especially if you're going to offer them housing when they accept a job in Hard Luck."

"You'd better throw in some land while you're at it," Ben said, reaching for the coffeepot. He refilled the mugs and set the pot back on the burner. "You O'Hallorans got far more of it than you know what to do with. Offer the women a cabin and twenty acres of land if

44

they'll live and work in Hard Luck for one year."

"Great idea!"

"Just like the old days when the settlers first got here."

"Those cabins aren't *on* any twenty acres." Sawyer raised his arms to stop the discussion. "It'd be misleading to let anyone think they were, or that —"

"No one said the cabins had to be on acreage, did they?" Duke broke in. "Besides, to my way of thinking, people shouldn't look a gift house in the mouth." He chuckled at his own feeble joke. "House, get it? Not horse."

"A year sounds fair," Christian said decisively, ignoring him. "If it doesn't work out, then they're free to leave, no hard feelings."

"No hard feelings." John nodded happily.

"Now, just a minute," Sawyer said. Was he the only one here who possessed any sense? He'd come into the Hard Luck Café for a simple cup of coffee, discouraged by the news that Phil was leaving. The morning had rapidly gone from bad to worse.

"How are we going to let women know about your offer?" Ralph asked.

"We'll run some ads like we said," Christian told him. "But maybe not in magazines. That'll take too long. I've got a business trip planned to Seattle, so we can put ads in the papers there and I'll interview the women who apply."

"Hold on," Sawyer said, frowning. "We can't go giving away those cabins, never mind the acreage, without talking to Charles first. Besides, there are antidiscrimination laws that make it illegal to advertise a job for women only."

Christian grinned. "There're ways around that."

Sawyer rolled his eyes. "But we really do need to discuss this with Charles." Their oldest brother was a silent partner in the O'Hallorans' air charter service. He should have a voice in this decision; after all, they'd be giving away family-owned cabins and land.

"There isn't time for that," Christian argued. "Charles'll go along with it. You know he will. He hasn't paid that much attention to the business since he started working for Alaska Oil."

"You'd better have an attorney draw up some kind of contract," Ben suggested.

"Right." Christian added that to his list. "I'll do it tomorrow. I'll write the ad this morning and see about getting it in the Seattle paper. It might be best if we placed it in another city, as well. It wouldn't be much trouble to go down to Oregon and interview women from Portland. I've got plenty of time."

"Hey, good idea," John murmured.

"I'll design the application," Sawyer said reluctantly. This was happening much too fast. "You know, guys . . ." He hated to throw another wrench in the works, but someone needed a clear head, and it was obvious he'd been elected. "If any woman's foolish enough to respond, those old cabins had better be in decent shape. It's going to take a lot of work."

"I'll help," John said enthusiastically.

"Me, too."

"I expect we all will." Duke drained the last of his coffee, then narrowed his gaze on Christian. "Just make sure you get a blonde for me."

"A blonde," Christian repeated.

Sawyer closed his eyes and

groaned. He had a bad feeling about this. A very bad feeling.

CHAPTER 1

It had been one of those days. Abbey Sutherland made herself a cup of tea, then sat in the large overstuffed chair and propped her feet on the ottoman. She closed her eyes, soaking in the silence.

The morning had started badly when Scott overslept, which meant he and Susan had missed the school bus. Seven-year-old Susan had insisted on wearing her pink sweater, which was still in the dirty-clothes hamper, and she'd whined all the way to school. Abbey had driven them, catching every red light en route.

By the time she arrived at the library, she was ten minutes late. Mrs. Duffy gave her a look that could have curdled milk.

But those minor irritations faded after lunch. Abbey received notice that the library's budget for the next fiscal year had been reduced and two positions would be cut — the positions held by the most recently hired employees. In other words, Abbey was going to lose her job in less than three months.

She finally got home at six o'clock, tired, short-tempered and depressed. That was when Mr. Erickson, the manager of the apartment complex, hand-delivered a note informing her the rents were being raised.

It was the kind of day even hot fudge couldn't salvage.

Sensing her mood, the kids had acted up all evening. Abbey was exhausted, and she didn't think reruns of *Matlock* were going to help.

Sipping her tea, she wondered what had happened to throw her life off course. She had a savings account, but there wasn't enough in it to pay more than a month's worth of bills. She refused to go to her parents for money. Not again. It had been too humiliating the first time, although they'd been eager to help. Not once had her mother or father said "I told you so," when she filed for divorce, although they'd issued plenty of warnings when she'd announced her intention to marry Dick Sutherland. They'd been right. Five years and two children later, Abbey had returned to Seattle emotionally battered, broken-hearted and just plain broke.

Her parents had helped her back on her feet despite their limited income and lent her money to finish her education. Abbey had painstakingly repaid every penny, but it had taken her almost three years.

The newspaper, still rolled up, lay at her feet, and she picked it up. She might as well start reading through the want ads now, although she wasn't likely to find another job as an assistant librarian. With cuts in local government spending, positions in libraries were becoming rare these days. But if she was willing to relocate . . .

"Mom." Scott stood beside her chair.

"Yes?" She climbed out of her depression long enough to manage a smile for her nine-year-old son.

"Jason's dog had her puppies."

Abbey felt her chest tighten. Scott had been asking for a dog all year. "Honey, we've already been over this a hundred times. The apartment complex doesn't allow pets."

"I didn't say I wanted one," he said defensively. "All I said was that Jason's dog had puppies. I know I can't have a dog as long as we live here, but I was thinking that maybe with the rent increase we might move."

"And if we do move," Abbey said, "you want me to look for a place where we can have a dog."

Her son grinned broadly. "Jason's puppies are really, really cute, Mom. And they're valuable, too! But you know what kind are my favorite?"

She did, but she played along. "Tell me."

"Huskies."

"Because the University of Washington mascot is a husky."

"Yeah. They have cool eyes, don't they? And I really like the way their tails loop up. I know they're too big for me to have as a pet, but I still like them best."

Abbey held out her arm to her son. He didn't cuddle with her much anymore. That was kid stuff to a boy who was almost ten. But tonight he seemed willing to forget that.

He clambered into the chair next to her, rested his head against her shoulder and sighed. "I'm sorry I overslept this morning," he whispered.

"I'm sorry I yelled at you."

"That's all right." There was a pause. "I promise to get out of bed when you call from now on, okay?"

"Okay." Abbey closed her eyes, breathing in the clean shampoo scent of his hair.

They sat together for a few more minutes, saying nothing.

"You'd better get back to bed," Abbey said, although she was reluctant to see him go.

Scott climbed out of the chair. "Are we going to move?" he asked, looking at her with wide eyes.

"I guess we are," she said and smiled.

" 'Night, Mom." Scott smiled, too, then walked down the hall to his bedroom.

Abbey's heart felt a little lighter as she picked up the paper and peeled off the rubber band. She didn't bother to look at the front page, but turned directly to the classifieds.

The square box with the large

block printing attracted her attention immediately. "LONELY MEN IN HARD LUCK, ALASKA, OFFER JOBS, HOMES AND LAND." Below in smaller print was a list of the positions open.

Abbey's heart stopped when she saw "librarian."

Hard Luck, Alaska. Jobs. A home with land. Twenty acres. Good grief, that was more than her grandfather had owned when he grew raspberries in Puyallup a generation earlier.

Dragging out an atlas, Abbey flipped through the pages until she found Alaska. Her finger ran down the list of town names until she came across Hard Luck. Population 150.

She swallowed. A small town generally meant a sense of community. That excited her. As a girl, she'd spent summers on her grandparents' farm and loved it. She wanted to give her children the same opportunity. She was sure the three of them could adjust to life in a small town. In Alaska.

Using the atlas's directions to locate the town, Abbey drew her finger across one side of the page and down the other.

Her excitement died. Hard Luck was above the Arctic Circle. Oh, dear. Maybe it *wasn't* such a great idea, after all.

The following morning, Abbey reviewed her options.

She set out a box of cold cereal, along with a carton of milk. A still-sleepy Scott and Susan pulled out chairs and sat at the table.

"Kids," she said, drawing a deep breath, "what would you say if I suggested we move to Alaska?"

"Alaska?" Scott perked up right away. "That's where they have huskies!"

"Yes, I know."

"It's cold there, isn't it?" Susan asked.

"Very cold. Colder than it's ever been in Seattle."

"Colder than Texas?"

"Lots colder," Scott said in a superior older-brother tone. "It's so cold you don't even need refrigerators, isn't that right, Mom?"

"Uh, I think they probably still use them."

"But they wouldn't need to if they didn't have electricity. Right?"

"Right."

"Could I have a dog there?"

Abbey weighed her answer carefully. "We'd have to find that out after we arrived."

"Would Grandma and Grandpa come and visit?" Susan asked.

"I'm sure they would, and if they didn't, we could visit them."

Scott poured cereal into his bowl until it threatened to spill over.

"I read an ad in the paper last night. Hard Luck, Alaska, needs a librarian, and it looks like I'm going to need a new job soon."

Scott and Susan didn't comment.

"I didn't think it would be fair to call and ask for an interview without discussing it with both of you first."

"You should go for it," Scott advised, but Abbey could see visions of huskies in her son's bright blue eyes.

"It'll mean a big change for all of us."

"Is there snow all the time?" Susan wanted to know.

"I don't think so, but I'll ask." Abbey hesitated, wondering exactly how much she should tell her children. "The ad said the job comes with a cabin and twenty acres of land."

The spoon was poised in front of Scotty's mouth. "To keep?"

Abbey nodded. "But we'd need to live there for a year. I imagine there won't be many applicants, but then I don't know. There doesn't seem to be an abundance of jobs for assistant librarians, either."

"I could live anywhere for a year. Go for it, Mom!"

"Susan?" Abbey suspected the decision would be more difficult for her daughter.

"Will there be girls my age?"

"Probably, but I can't guarantee that. The town only has 150 people, and it would be very different from the life we have here in Seattle."

"Come on, Susan," Scott urged. "We could have our very own house."

Susan's small shoulders heaved in a great sigh. "Do *you* want to move, Mommy?"

Abbey stroked her daughter's hair. Call her greedy. Call her materialistic. Call her a sucker, but she couldn't stop thinking about those twenty acres and that cabin. No mortgage. Land. Security. And a job she loved. All in Hard Luck, Alaska.

She inhaled deeply, then nodded.

"Then I guess it would be all right."

Scott let out a holler and leapt from his chair. He grabbed Abbey's hands and they danced around the room.

"I haven't got the job yet," Abbey cried, breathless.

"But you'll get it," Scott said confidently.

Abbey hoped her son was right.

CHAPTER 2

Abbey took several calming breaths before walking up to the hotel desk and giving her name.

"Mr. O'Halloran's taking interviews in the Snoqualmie Room on the second floor," the clerk told her.

Abbey's fingers tightened around her résumé as she headed for the escalator. Her heart pounded heavily, feeling like a lead weight in her chest.

Her decision to apply for this position had understandably received mixed reactions. Both Scott and Susan were excited about the prospect of a new life in Hard Luck, but Abbey's parents were hesitant.

Marie Murray would miss spoiling her grandchildren. Abbey's father, Wayne, was convinced she didn't know what she'd be getting into moving to the frozen north. But he seemed to forget that she made her living in a library. Soon after placing the initial call, Abbey had checked out a number of excellent books about life in Alaska. Her research had told her everything she wanted to know — and more.

Nevertheless, she'd already decided to accept the job if it was offered. No matter how cold the winters were, living in Hard Luck would be better than having to accept money from her parents.

Abbey found the Snoqualmie Room easily enough and glanced inside. A lean, rawboned man in his early thirties sat at a table reading intently. The hotel staff must have thought applicants would arrive thirsty, because they'd supplied a pitcher of ice water and at least two dozen glasses.

"Hello," she said with a polite smile. "I'm Abbey Sutherland."

"Abbey." The man stood abruptly as if she'd caught him unawares. "I'm Christian O'Halloran. We spoke on the phone." He motioned to the seat on the other side of the table. "Make yourself comfortable."

She sat and handed him her résumé.

He barely looked at it before setting it aside. "Thank you. I'll read this later."

Abbey nervously folded her hands in her lap and waited.

"You're applying for the position of librarian, right?"

"Yes. I'm working toward my degree in library science."

"In other words, you're not a full librarian."

"That's correct. In Washington state, a librarian is required to have a master's degree in library science. For the last two years I've worked as an assistant librarian for King County." She paused. Christian O'Halloran was difficult to read. "I answer reference questions, do quick information retrieval and customer service, and of course I have computer skills." She hesitated, wondering if she should continue.

"That sounds perfect. Hard Luck doesn't exactly have a library at the moment. We do have a building of sorts. . . ."

"Books?"

"Oh, yes, hundreds of those. At least a thousand. They were a gift to the town, and we need someone who's capable of handling every aspect of organizing a library."

"I'd be fully capable of that." She listed a number of responsibilities she'd handled in her job with the King County library system. Somehow, though, Abbey couldn't shake the feeling that Christian O'Halloran wasn't really interested in hearing about her qualifications.

He mentioned the pay, and although it wasn't as much as she was earning with King County, she wouldn't need to worry about rent.

A short silence followed, almost as if he wasn't sure what else to ask.

"Could you tell me a little about the library building?" she ventured.

He nodded. "Actually it was a home at one time — my grandfather's original homestead, in fact — but I don't think you'd have much of a problem turning it into a library, would you?"

"Probably not."

Already, Abbey's mind was at

work, dividing up the house. One of the bedrooms could be used for fiction, another for nonfiction. The dining room would be perfect for a reading room, or it could be set up as an area for children.

"You understand that life in Hard Luck isn't going to be anything like Seattle," Christian commented, breaking into her thoughts.

Her father had said that very thing the day before. "I realize that." She paused for a moment. "Could I ask you about the house and the land you're offering?"

"Of course."

"Well, uh, could you tell me about the house?"

She waited.

"It's more of a cabin, and I'd

describe it as . . . rustic." He seemed to stumble on the word. "It definitely has a . . . rural feel. Don't get me wrong, it's comfortable, but it's different from what you're used to."

"I'm sure it is. Tell me about Hard Luck."

The man across from her relaxed. "It's probably the most beautiful place on earth. You might think I'm prejudiced and I can't very well deny it. I guess you'll have to form your own opinion.

"In summer there's sunlight nearly twenty-four hours a day. That's when the wildflowers bloom. I swear every color under the sun bursts to life almost overnight. The forests and tundra turn scarlet and gold and burnt orange."

"It sounds lovely." And it did. "What about the winters?"

"Oh, yes. Well, again, it's beautiful, but the beauty is kind of . . . stark. Pristine's a good word. I don't think anyone's really lived until they've seen our light show."

"The aurora borealis."

Christian smiled approvingly. "I'm not going to lie to you," he continued. "It gets mighty cold. In winter it isn't uncommon for the temperature to drop to forty or fifty below."

"My goodness." Although Abbey knew this, hearing him say it reinforced the reality.

"On those days, almost everything closes down. We don't generally fly when it's that cold. It's too hard on the planes, and even harder on the pilots."

Abbey nodded; he'd told her about Midnight Sons, the O'Halloran brothers' air charter service, during their phone conversation.

"What about everything else?" she asked. "Like the school. Does it close down, too?" He'd also explained in their previous conversation that Hard Luck had a school that went from kindergarten to twelfth grade.

"Life in town comes to a standstill, and we all sort of snuggle together. There's nothing to do in weather that cold but wait it out. Most days, we manage to keep the school open, though." He shrugged. "We rely on one another in Hard Luck. We have to."

"What about food?"

"We've got a grocery store. It's not a supermarket, mind you, but it carries the essentials. Everyone in town stocks up on supplies once a year. But if you run out of anything, there's always the grocery. If Pete Livengood — he's the guy who owns it — if he doesn't have what you need, one of the pilots can pick it up for you. Midnight Sons makes daily flights into Fairbanks, so it isn't like you're stuck there."

"What about driving to Fairbanks? When I looked up Hard Luck, I couldn't make out any roads. There is one, isn't there?"

"Sure there is — in a manner of speaking," Christian said proudly. "We got ourselves a haul road a few years back."

Abbey was relieved. If she did get the job, she'd have to have her furniture and other household effects delivered; without a road, that would obviously have been a problem. Flying them was sure to be prohibitively expensive.

"Do you have any more questions for me?" she asked.

"None." Christian looked at his watch. "Would you mind filling out the application form while you're here? I'll be holding interviews for the next day or so. I'll call you tomorrow afternoon, if that's all right."

Abbey stood. "That'd be fine."

Christian gave her the one-page application, which she completed quickly and gave back to him.

He rose from behind the table and extended his hand. "It was a pleasure to meet you."

"You, too." Even before she'd come in for the interview, she'd known she'd accept the position if it was offered to her. She needed a job, needed to support her family. If that meant traveling to the ends of the earth, she'd do it. But as she turned to walk away, Abbey realized she not only needed this position, she *wanted* it. Badly.

She loved the idea of creating her own library. But it wasn't just the challenge of the job that excited her. She'd watched this man's eyes light up as he talked about his home. When he said Hard Luck was beautiful, he'd said it with sincerity, with passion. When he told her about the tundra and the forest, she could imagine their beauty. She'd seen plenty of photographs and even a *National Geographic* documentary, but it was his words that truly convinced her. More than that, *excited* her.

"Mr. O'Halloran?" she said, surprising herself.

He was already seated, leafing intently through a sheaf of papers. He glanced up. "Yes?"

"If you decide to hire me, I promise I'll do a good job for you and the people in Hard Luck."

He nodded. "And I promise I'll phone you soon."

"Well?" Scott looked at Abbey expectantly when she walked into the house. "How'd the interview go?"

Abbey slipped off her pumps and curled her toes into the carpet. "Fine — I think."

"Will you get the job?"

Abbey didn't want to build up her son's hopes. "I don't know, honey. Where's Missy?" Since she paid the teenage babysitter top dollar, she expected her to stay with Scott and Susan for the agreed-upon number of hours.

"Her mother wanted her to put a

roast in the oven at four-thirty. Susan went with her. They'll be back soon."

Abbey collapsed into her favorite chair and dangled her arms over the sides. Her feet rested on the ottoman.

"Are you finished your homework?" she asked.

"I don't have any. There's only a couple more weeks left of school."

"I know."

Abbey dreaded the summer months. Every year, day camp and babysitting were more and more expensive. Scott was getting old enough to resent having a teenager stay with him. Not that Abbey blamed him. Before she knew it, her son would be thirteen himself.

"Would it be okay if I went over to Jason's house?" he asked eagerly. "I'll be home in time for dinner."

Abbey nodded, but she knew it wasn't the other boy he was interested in seeing. It was those puppies that'd captured his nine-year-old heart.

Sawyer walked into the long, narrow structure that sat next to the gravel-and-dirt runway. The mobile served as the office for Midnight Sons. Eventually they hoped to build a real office. That had been on the agenda for the past eight years — ever since they'd started the business. During those years, Charles and Sawyer had built their own homes. Sawyer's was across the street from Christian's place, which had been the O'Halloran family home. Charles's house was one street over — not that there were paved streets in Hard Luck.

But they'd been too busy running Midnight Sons — flying cargo and passengers, hiring pilots, negotiating contracts and all the other myriad responsibilities that came with a business like theirs. Constructing an office building was just another one of those things they hadn't gotten around to doing.

Exhausted, Sawyer threw himself down on the hard-backed swivel chair at Christian's desk. Cleaning those old cabins was proving to be hard work. Much more of this, he thought ruefully, and he was going to end up with dishpan hands.

He'd been astonished — and impressed — by the willingness of their pilots to pitch in and make those old cabins livable. One thing was for sure; the log structures were solid. A few minor repairs, lots of soapy water and a little attention had done wonders. Not that a forty-year-old log cabin was going to impress a city girl. More than likely, the women Christian hired would take one look at those shacks and book the next flight south.

The phone pealed and Sawyer reached for it. As he did, he noticed the message light blinking.

"Midnight Sons."

"Where have you been all day?"

Christian grumbled. "I've left three messages. I've been sitting here waiting for you to call me back."

"Sorry," Sawyer muttered, biting back the temptation to offer to trade places. While Christian was gallivanting all over kingdom come securing airplane parts, talking to travel agents, *meeting women* and generally having a good time, Sawyer had been wielding a mop and pail. In Sawyer's opinion, his younger brother had gotten the better end of this deal. As for himself, he'd seen enough cobwebs in the past week to last him a lifetime.

"You can tell Duke I found him a blonde," Christian announced triumphantly. "Her name's Allison Reynolds, and she's going to be our secretary — well, maybe."

Sawyer's jaw tightened as he made an effort to hold back his irritation. "What're her qualifications?"

"You mean other than being blond?" Christian asked, then chuckled. "I'm telling you, Sawyer, I've never seen anything like this in my life. I placed the ad in the Seattle paper, and the answering service has been swamped. There are a lot of lonely women in this world."

"Does our new secretary know she'll be living in a log cabin *without* the comforts of home?"

"Naturally I told her about the cabin, but, uh, I didn't have a chance to go into all the details."

"Christian! That's hardly a detail. She'll be expecting to see modern plumbing, not a path to the outhouse. Women don't like that kind of surprise."

"I didn't want to scare her off," he argued.

"She deserves the truth."

"I know, I know. Actually I offered her the position and she's thinking it over. If she decides to accept the job, I'll give her more information."

"You mean to tell me that out of all the women who applied, you chose one who isn't even sure she wants the job?" Sawyer didn't often fly off the handle, but his brother was annoying him more than usual.

"Trust me, Allison wants the position," Christian insisted. "She just needs to think about it. I would, too, in the circumstances." He paused. "Our ad certainly attracted a lot of attention."

Sawyer had carefully gone over the ad they'd submitted to the Seattle and Portland papers. He'd been concerned that they not inadvertently put in anything that might be misleading or violate the antidiscrimination laws. So there was nothing in the ad to suggest a man couldn't apply. No one wanted to deal with a lawsuit a few weeks down the road.

"I must've talked to at least thirty women in the past couple of days," Christian said, his voice ringing with enthusiasm. "And there were that many more phone inquiries."

"What about a librarian? Has anyone applied for that?"

"A few, but not nearly as many as for the position of secretary. The minute I met Allison —"

"Does she type?"

"She must," Christian answered. "She works in an office."

"Didn't you give her a test?" Sawyer asked, not bothering to conceal his disgust.

"What for? It isn't like she'll need a hundred words a minute, is it?"

Sawyer rubbed his face. "I can't believe I'm hearing this."

"Wait until you meet her, Sawyer," Christian said happily. "She's a knockout."

"Oh, great." He could picture it

already. His crew would be hanging around the office, tongues hanging out over a dizzy blonde, instead of flying. Midnight Sons didn't need this kind of trouble.

"Don't worry about it," his brother said. "I've made a lot of progress. You should be pleased."

"It doesn't sound like you've done much of anything." Sawyer was fuming. He'd hoped — obviously a futile hope — that Christian would use a bit of common sense.

"Listen, I haven't made up my mind which woman to hire for our librarian. There were a couple of excellent applicants."

"Any blondes?" Sawyer asked sarcastically.

"Yeah, one, but she looked too fragile to last. I liked her, though. There's another one who seemed to really want the job. It makes me wonder why she'd leave a cushy job here in Seattle for Hard Luck. It's not like we're offering great benefits."

"But a house and twenty acres *sounds* like a lot," Sawyer said from between clenched teeth.

"You think I should hire her?"

He sighed. "If she's qualified and she wants the job, then by all means, hire her."

"Okay. I'll give her a call as soon as we're finished and make the arrangements."

"Just a minute." Sawyer shoved one hand through his hair. "Is she pretty?" He was quickly losing faith in his brother's judgment. Christian had already decided on a secretary, and he didn't know if she could so much as file. Heaven help them all if he hired the rest of the applicants based on their looks rather than their qualifications.

Christian hesitated. "I suppose you could say the librarian's pretty, but she isn't going to bowl you over the way Allison will. She's just sort of regular pretty. Brown hair and eyes, average height. Cute upturned nose.

"Now with Allison, well, there's no comparison. We're talking sexy here. Wait until John gets a look at her . . . front," Christian said, and chuckled. "She's swimsuit-issue material."

"Hire her!" Sawyer snapped.

"Allison? I already have, but she wants twenty-four hours to think it over. I told you that."

"I meant the *librarian.*"

"Oh, all right, if you think I should."

Sawyer propped his elbows on the desk and shook his head. "Anything else you called to tell me about?"

"Not much. I'm not doing any more interviews for now. Allison and the librarian, plus the new teacher, that's three — enough to start with. Let's see how things work out. I've collected a couple of dozen résumés, and I'll save them for future reference. Unless I find a cook for Ben or —"

"Don't hire any more," Sawyer insisted. He was well aware that he sounded short-tempered, but frankly he was and he didn't care if his brother knew it.

"Oh, yeah, I meant to tell you. If Allison does take the job, she won't be able to start right away. Apparently she's booked a vacation with a friend. I told her that's okay. We've waited this long. Another couple of weeks won't matter."

"Why don't you ask her if next year would be convenient?"

"Very funny. What's wrong with you? I get the feeling you're envious — not that I blame you. I wish we'd thought of this a long time ago. Meeting and talking to all these women is a lot of fun. See you."

The phone went dead in Sawyer's hand.

Abbey's spirits were low. Dragging-in-the-gutter low. She hadn't got the job. O'Halloran would've phoned by now if he'd decided to hire her.

Scott and Susan, ever sensitive to her moods, pushed their dinner around their plates. No one seemed to have much of an appetite.

"It doesn't look like I got the job in Alaska," she told them. There wasn't any reason to keep her children's hopes alive. "Mr. O'Halloran, the man who interviewed me, was supposed to call this afternoon if he'd chosen me."

"That's all right, Mom," Scott said with a brave smile. "You'll find something else."

"I wanted to go to Alaska," Susan said, her lower lip trembling. "I told everyone at school we were moving."

"We are." Abbey knew this was of little comfort, but she threw it in, anyway. "It just so happens that we won't be moving to Alaska."

"Can we visit there someday?" Scott asked. "I liked what we read in those books you brought home. It seems like a great place."

"Someday." *Someday,* Abbey realized, could be a magical word, filled with the promise of a brighter tomorrow. At the moment, though, it just sounded bleak.

The phone rang, and both Susan and Scott twisted around, looking eagerly at the kitchen wall. Neither of them moved. Abbey didn't allow the dinner hour to be interrupted by phone calls.

"The machine will pick up the message," she told them unnecessarily.

After the fourth ring, the answering machine automatically clicked on. Everyone went still, straining to hear who'd phoned.

"This is Christian O'Halloran."

"Mom!" Scott cried excitedly.

Abbey flew across the kitchen, ripping the phone off the hook. "Mr. O'Halloran," she said breathlessly, "hello."

"Hello," Christian responded.

"I'm glad I caught you."

"I'm glad you caught me, too. Have you made your decision?" She hated to sound so eager, but she couldn't stop herself.

"You've got the job, if you still want it."

"I do," Abbey said, giving Scott and Susan a thumbs-up. Her son and daughter stabbed triumphant fists in the air.

"When can you start?"

Abbey was certain the library would let her leave with minimal notice. "Whenever it's convenient for you."

"How about next week?" Christian asked. "I won't return from my business trip until the end of the month, but I'll arrange for my brother Sawyer to meet you in Fairbanks."

"*Next* week?"

"Is that too soon?"

"No, no," she said quickly, fearing he might change his mind. She could take the kids out of school a week early, and she wouldn't need much time to pack their belongings. Her mother would help, and whatever they didn't take with them on the plane — like their furniture — she could have shipped later.

"I'll see you in Hard Luck, then."

"Thank you. I can't tell you how pleased I am," she said. "Oh, before I hang up . . ." she began, thinking she should probably mention the fact that she'd be bringing Scott and Susan. Despite the provision of housing, there was nothing on the application asking about children or family.

"I'll be with you in a minute, Allison," Christian said.

"Excuse me?"

"My dinner date just arrived," he told her. "As I explained, my brother will meet you in Fairbanks. I'll have the travel agency call you to make the arrangements for your ticket."

"You're paying my airfare?"

"Of course. And don't worry about packing for the winter. You can buy what you need once you arrive."

"But —"

"I wish I had more time to answer

your questions," he said distract-
edly. "Sawyer's really the one who
can tell you what you need to
know."

"Mr. O'Halloran —"

"Good luck, Abbey."

"Thank you." She gave up trying.
He'd learn about Scott and Susan
when he returned. As far as she was
concerned, the town was getting a
great librarian — plus a bonus!

"You sure you don't want me to fly
in and meet the new librarian this
afternoon?" John Henderson asked,
straddling the chair across from
Sawyer. His hair had been dampened and combed down, and it
looked as if he was wearing a new
shirt.

"Be my guest." You'd think the Queen of England was flying in judging by the way folks in Hard Luck were behaving. Duke had arrived at Ben's this morning clean-shaven and spiffed up, smelling pungently of aftershave. Sawyer hid a grin. The next woman would follow in a few days, and he wondered how long it would take for everyone to get tired of these welcoming parties.

"You'll let John pick up the new librarian over my dead body," Duke barked. "We all know what happened the last time he flew a woman into Hard Luck."

"I keep telling you that wasn't my fault."

"Forget it! I'll pick her up." Sawyer looked away from his squabbling pilots in disgust and happened to notice the blackboard where Ben wrote out the daily lunch and dinner specials.

"Beef Wellington?" he asked.

"You got a problem with Beef Wellington?" Ben muttered belligerently. "I'm just trying to show our new librarian that we're a civilized bunch."

In Sawyer's opinion, this whole project didn't show a lot of promise. He'd bet none of these women would last the winter. The bad feeling he'd experienced when they first discussed the idea had returned tenfold.

"You talk to that Seattle paper yet?" Ben asked, setting a plate of scrambled eggs and toast in front of him.

"No." Sawyer frowned. The press was becoming a problem. It wasn't surprising that the media had gotten hold of the situation and wanted to do stories on it. They'd been hounding Sawyer for interviews all week — thanks to Christian, who'd given out his name. He was damn near ready to throttle his younger brother. And he was sorely tempted to have the phone disconnected; if it wasn't vital for business, he swore he would've done it already.

Now that the first woman was actually arriving, Sawyer regretted not discussing The Plan with their oldest brother. Although Charles was a full partner in the flight service, he was employed as a surveyor for Alaska Oil and was often away from Hard Luck for weeks on end. Like right now.

When he did get home, Charles would probably think they'd all lost their minds. Sawyer wouldn't blame him, either.

"Well, the cabin's ready, anyway," Duke said with satisfaction.

After they'd scrubbed down the walls and floors, Sawyer and a few of the men had opened up the storeroom in the lodge and dug out some of the old furniture. Sawyer had expressed doubts about sleeping on mattresses that had been tucked away for so many years, but Pearl and various other women —

including several who were wives of pipeline maintenance workers — had aired everything out. They'd assured him that aside from some lingering mustiness, there was nothing to worry about. Everything had been well wrapped in plastic.

As much as Sawyer hated to admit it, the cabin looked almost inviting. The black potbellied stove gleamed from repeated scrubbing. The women had sewn floral curtains for the one window and a matching tablecloth for the rough wooden table. The townspeople had stacked the shelves with groceries, and someone had even donated a cooler to keep perishables fresh for a few days. The single bed, made up with sun-dried linens and one thin blanket, did resemble something one might find in a prison, but Sawyer didn't say so. Pearl and her friends had worked hard to make the cabin as welcoming as possible.

When he'd stopped there on his way to Ben's for breakfast, he saw that someone had placed a Mason jar of freshly cut wildflowers on the table. Right beside the kerosene lantern and the can opener.

Well, this was as good as it got.

"How are you going to know it's her when she steps off the plane?" Ben asked, standing directly in front of him and watching him eat.

"I'm wearing my Midnight Sons jacket," Sawyer answered. "I'll let her figure it out."

"What's her name again?"

"Abbey Sutherland."

"I bet she's pretty," Duke muttered.

His pilots gazed sightlessly into the distance, longing written on their faces. Sawyer wouldn't have believed it if he hadn't seen it with his own eyes.

"I'm getting out of here before you three make me lose my breakfast."

"You sure you don't want me to ride along with you?" John asked hopefully.

"I'm sure." Sawyer would also be bringing back the mail and a large order of canned goods for the grocery. He was flying the Baron, and he sincerely hoped Abbey Sutherland had packed light. He didn't have room for more than two suit-cases, and he intended to store those in the nose.

Grabbing his jacket from the back of the chair, Sawyer headed out the door and across Hard Luck's main street toward the runway.

He could've flown into Fairbanks with his eyes closed, he'd made the flight so often. He landed, took care of loading up the mail and other freight, then — with a sense of dread — made his way to the terminal.

After checking the monitor to make sure the flight was coming in on time, Sawyer bought a coffee and ventured out to the assigned gate.

He was surprised by how busy the terminal was. Tourists, he guessed. Not that he was complaining. They brought a lot of money into the state. Not as much as oil did, of course, but they certainly repre-sented a healthy part of the economy.

Even the airport was geared to-ward impressing tourists, he noted. The first thing many saw when they walked in was a massive mounted polar bear, rearing up on its hind legs. Although he'd seen it a hun-dred times, Sawyer still felt awed by it.

The plane arrived on schedule. Sipping coffee, Sawyer waited for the passengers to enter the termi-nal.

He glanced at each one, not knowing what to expect. Christian's description of Abbey Sutherland sure left something to be desired. From what he remembered, Christian had said she was "regular" pretty.

Every woman he saw seemed to match that description, such as it was. With the exception of one.

She was probably in her early thirties. She had two kids at her side. The little girl, who couldn't have been more than six or seven, clutched a stuffed bear. The boy, perhaps two or three years older, looked as if he needed a leash to hold him back. The kid was raring to go.

The woman wasn't *pretty*, Sawyer

decided, she was downright lovely. Her glossy brown hair was short and straight and fell to just below her ears. Her eyes skirted past him. He liked their warm brown color and he liked her calm manner.

He also liked the way she protectively drew her children close as she looked around. She too, it seemed, was seeking someone.

With a determined effort, Sawyer pulled his gaze away from her and scanned the crowd for Christian's librarian.

Brown hair and cute upturned nose.

He found himself looking back at the woman with the two children. Their eyes met, and her generous mouth formed a smile. It wasn't a shy smile or a coy one. It was open and friendly, as if she recognized him and expected him to recognize her.

Then she walked right over to him. "Hello," she said.

"Hello." Fearing he'd miss the woman he'd come to meet, his eyes slid past her to the people still disembarking from the plane.

"I'm Abbey Sutherland."

Sawyer's gaze shot back to her before dropping to the two kids.

"These are my children, Scott and Susan," she said. "Thank you for meeting us."

CHAPTER 3

"Your children?" Sawyer repeated.

"Yes," Abbey said. It was easy to see the family resemblance between Sawyer and Christian O'Halloran, she thought. Both were tall and lean and rawboned. If he'd lived a hundred years earlier, he could've been on horseback, riding across some now-forgotten range in the Old West. Instead, he was flying over a large expanse of wilderness, from one fringe of civilization to another.

Whereas Christian had been clean-shaven, Sawyer had a beard. The dark hair suited his face. His eyes were a pale shade of gray-blue, not unlike those of a husky, Scott's favorite dog. He wore a red-checked flannel shirt under a jacket marked with the Midnight Sons logo. She suspected he had no idea how attractive he was.

"Hi," Scott said eagerly, looking up at Sawyer.

The pilot held out his hand and she noticed that his eyes softened as he exchanged handshakes with her son. "Pleased to meet you, Scott."

"Alaska sure is big."

"That it is. Hello, Susan," Sawyer said next, holding out his hand to her daughter. The girl solemnly shook it, then glanced at Abbey and smiled, clearly delighted with this gesture of grown-up respect.

"Could we speak privately, Ms. Sutherland?" Sawyer asked. The warmth and welcome vanished from his eyes as he motioned toward the waiting area. He walked just far enough away so the children couldn't hear him. Abbey followed, keeping a close eye on Scott and Susan.

"Christian didn't mention that you have children," Sawyer said without preamble.

"He didn't ask. And there was no reference to family on the application or the agreement Christian sent me. I did think it was a bit odd not to inquire about my circumstances, considering that you're providing housing."

"You might've said something." An accusatory look tightened his mouth.

"I didn't get a chance," she explained in even tones. His attitude was beginning to irritate her. "I did try, but he was busy, and I really didn't think it would matter."

"There's nothing in the agreement about children."

"I'm aware of that," Abbey said, striving to keep the emotion out of her voice. "As I already told you, I filled out the application and answered every question, and there wasn't a single one about dependants. Frankly, I don't think they're anyone's concern but mine. I was hired as a librarian. And as long as I do my job, I —"

"That's right, but —"

"I really can't see that it matters whether or not I have a family to support."

"What about your husband?"

"I'm divorced. Listen, would you mind if we discussed this another time? The children and I are exhausted. We landed in Anchorage late last night and were up early this morning to catch the connecting flight to Fairbanks. Would it be too much to ask that we wait for a more opportune moment to sort this out?"

He hesitated, then said in crisp tones, "No problem."

The pulse in his temple throbbed visibly, and Abbey suspected that it was, in fact, very much of a problem.

"I brought the Baron," he said, directing the three of them toward the luggage carousel. "All I can say is I hope you packed light."

Abbey wasn't sure how she was supposed to interpret "packed light." Everything she and the children owned that would fit was crammed into their suitcases. Everything that hadn't gone into their luggage had been sold, given away or handed over to a shipping company and would arrive within the month. She hoped.

"Look, Mom," Scott said, pointing at the wall where a variety of stuffed animals were displayed. Abbey shuddered, but her son's eyes remained fixed on the head of a huge brown bear. Its teeth were bared threateningly.

"That silly bear stuck his head right through the wall," Sawyer joked.

Scott laughed, but Susan stared hard as if that just might be possible.

When they'd collected all the luggage, Sawyer stepped back, frowning. "You brought *six* suitcases."

"Yes, I know," Abbey said calmly. "We needed six suitcases."

"I don't have room for all those in the plane. I'm not even sure how I'm going to get you, two kids, the mail and the rest of the cargo inside, much less enough luggage to sink a battleship. If you'd let me know, I could've brought a larger plane."

Abbey bit back a sarcastic reply. She'd *tried* to tell Christian about her children, but he'd been too interested in his dinner date to listen to her. She hadn't purposely hidden anything from him or Sawyer. And, good grief, how was *she* supposed to know how much luggage some airplane would hold?

"Never mind," Sawyer grumbled impatiently, "I'll figure it out later. Let's get going."

Abbey would've liked something to eat, but it was clear Sawyer was anxious to be on his way. Fortunately Scott and Susan, unlike their mother, had gobbled down what the airline laughably called a meal.

They loaded everything into the bed of a pickup and drove around the airport to a back road, which took them to an area used by various flight service operators.

"All that stuff belongs to Mom and Susan," Scott whispered conspiratorially as Sawyer helped him out of the cab. "They're the ones who insisted on bringing *everything.*"

"Sounds just like a couple of women," Sawyer muttered. He led them to the plane.

Abbey wasn't sure what she'd expected, but this compact dual-engine aircraft wasn't it. She peeked inside and realized that what Sawyer had said was true. There was barely room for her, let alone the children and all their luggage.

"There's only three seats," she said, looking nervously at Sawyer. It didn't take a mathematical genius to figure out that three seats wasn't enough for four people.

"You'll have to sit on my desk — the seat beside mine," Sawyer instructed after climbing aboard the aircraft. "And I'll buckle the kids together on the other seat."

"Is that legal?"

"Probably not in the lower forty-eight," he told her, "but we do it here. Don't worry, they'll be fine." He moved toward the cockpit, retrieved a black binder and a stack of papers from the passenger seat and crammed them into the space between the two seats.

"Go on in and sit down," he said, "while I see to the kids."

Abbey climbed awkwardly inside and carefully edged her way forward. By the time she fastened the seat belt, she was breathless.

Sawyer settled Scott and Susan in the remaining seat behind her. One look at her children told Abbey neither was pleased with the arrangement. But it couldn't be avoided.

"What about our luggage?" she asked when Sawyer slipped into the seat next to her.

He placed earphones over his head, then reached for the binder and made a notation in it.

"Our luggage?" she repeated.

"The suitcases don't fit. We're going to have to leave them behind."

"What?" Abbey cried. "We can't do that!"

Sawyer ignored her and continued to ready the plane for takeoff.

"How long is the flight?" Scott asked.

"About an hour."

"Can I fly the plane?"

"Not this time," Sawyer responded absently.

"*Later* can I?"

"We'll see."

"Mr. O'Halloran," Abbey said with a heavy sigh, "could we please discuss the luggage situation?"

"No. My contract is to deliver the

mail. That's far more important. I'm not going to unload cargo for a bunch of silly female things you aren't going to need, anyway."

Abbey gritted her teeth. "I didn't bring silly female things. Now if you'd kindly —"

Sawyer turned around and looked at Scott. "Do you like dogs?"

Scott's eyes grew huge. "You bet I do," he answered breathlessly.

Sawyer adjusted some switches. "When we get to Hard Luck, I'll take you over to meet Eagle Catcher."

"Is he a husky?"

"Yup."

"Really?" Scott sounded as if he'd died and gone to heaven. He was so excited it was a wonder he didn't bounce right out of the seat.

"Um, about our luggage?" Abbey hated to be a pest, but she didn't like being ignored, either. It might be unimportant to Buck Rogers here, but she'd rather they arrived in Hard Luck with something more than the clothes on their backs.

He didn't bother to answer. Instead, he started the engines and chatted in friendly tones with a man in the control tower. Come to think of it, he chatted in friendly tones with everyone but her.

Before Abbey could protest further, they were taxiing toward the runway.

In no time they were in the air. Above the roar of the twin engines, Abbey could hear nothing except the pounding of her heart. She'd never flown in a plane this small, and she closed her eyes and held on tightly as it pitched and heaved its way into the clear blue sky.

"Wow!" Scott shouted. "This is fun."

Abbey didn't share his reaction. Her stomach did a flip-flop as the plane banked sharply to one side. She braced her hands against the seat, muttering, "Come on! Straighten up and fly right, can't you?"

Still talking to the tower, Sawyer glanced at her and grinned. "Relax," he said. "I haven't been forced to crash-land in two or three months now."

"In other words, I haven't got a

thing to worry about." Abbey shouted to be heard above the engines. She peeked over her shoulder to be sure Scott and Susan weren't frightened. They weren't — quite the opposite. They smiled at her, thrilled with their first small-plane ride. She, on the other hand, preferred airplanes that came equipped with flight attendants.

Abbey wasn't able to make out much of the landscape below. She'd been disappointed earlier; during the flight from Anchorage to Fairbanks, Mount McKinley had been obscured by clouds. The pilot had announced that the highest mountain in North America was visible less than twenty percent of the time. He'd joked that perhaps it wasn't really there at all.

She glanced away from the window and back at Sawyer. He'd already demonstrated a fairly flexible attitude to safety rules, in her view. Now he took out the black binder he'd wedged between their seats and began to write. Abbey stared at him. Not once did his eyes shift from his task, whatever it was.

A light blinked repeatedly on the dashboard. Abbey knew nothing about small planes, but she figured if a light was blinking, there had to be a reason. They must be losing oil or gas or altitude or *something.*

When she couldn't stand it any longer, she gripped his arm and pointed to the light.

"Yes?" He looked at her blankly.

She didn't want to shout for fear of alarming her children, so she leaned her head as close to his as possible and said in a reasonable voice, "There's a light flashing."

"Yes, I see." He continued writing.

"Aren't you going to do something about it?"

"In a couple of minutes."

"I'd rather you took care of it now."

"There's nothing to worry about, Ms. Sutherland — Abbey," he said. Lines crinkled around his eyes, and he almost seemed to enjoy her discomfort. "All it indicates is that I'm on automatic pilot."

She felt like a fool. Crossing her arms, she wrapped what remained of her dignity about her and gazed out the window.

Sawyer tapped her on the shoulder. "You don't need to worry about your luggage, either. I've arranged with another flight service to have it delivered this afternoon."

He might have told her sooner, instead of leaving her to worry. "Thank you."

He nodded.

"What's that?" Scott shouted from behind her.

Abbey looked down to discover a streak of silver that stretched as far as the eye could see.

"That's the Alaska pipeline," Sawyer told Scott.

From the research she'd done on Alaska, Abbey knew that the pipeline traversed eight hundred miles of rugged mountain ranges, rivers and harsh terrain. It ran from Prudhoe Bay to Valdez, the northernmost ice-free port in North America.

Soon Abbey noticed that the plane was descending. She studied the landscape, trying to spot Hard Luck, excited about seeing the community that would be her home. She saw a row of buildings along one unpaved street, with a large structure set off to the side. Several other buildings were scattered about. She tried to count the houses and got to twenty before the plane lined up with the runway for its final descent.

As they drew close, Abbey realized the field wasn't paved, either. They were landing on what resembled a wide gravel road. She held her breath and braced herself as the wheels touched down, sure they'd hit hard against the rough ground. To her surprise, the landing was as smooth as any she'd experienced.

Sawyer cut the engine speed and taxied toward a mobile structure near the far end of the field. Abbey strained to see what she could out of the narrow side window. She smiled when she recognized a telephone booth. In the middle of the Arctic, at the very top of the world, it was comforting to know she could call home.

A burly man who resembled a

lumberjack barreled out of the mobile structure. Abbey lost sight of him, then heard the door on the side of the aircraft open.

"Howdy," he called, sticking his head and upper shoulders inside. "Welcome to Hard Luck. I'm John Henderson."

"Hello," Abbey called back.

John disappeared abruptly to be replaced by the head and shoulders of another outdoorsy-looking man. "I'm Ralph Ferris," he said. Three other faces crowded in around the opening.

"For crying out loud," Sawyer snapped, "would you guys let the passengers out of the plane first? This is ridiculous." He squeezed past her, unsnapped the seat belt secured around Scott and Susan and helped them out.

Abbey was the last person to disembark. As she moved down the three steps, she found all five men standing at attention, as if prepared for a military inspection. Their arms hung straight at their sides, their shoulders were squared, spines straight. If any of them were surprised to see two children, it didn't show.

Muttering to himself, Sawyer stalked past Abbey and into the mobile office, leaving her alone with her children. He slammed the door, apparently eager to be rid of them.

Abbey felt irritation swirl through her. How could he just abandon her? How could he be so *rude*? What had she done that was so terrible? Well, she could be rude, too!

"Welcome to Hard Luck." Her angry thoughts were swept aside as a tall, thin older woman with gray hair cut boyishly short stepped forward to greet her. "I'm Pearl Inman," she said, shaking Abbey's hand enthusiastically. "I can't tell you how pleased we are to have a librarian in Hard Luck."

"Thank you. These are my children, Scott and Susan. We're happy to be here." Abbey noted that Pearl seemed as unsurprised by the arrival of two children as the pilots were.

"You must be exhausted."

"We're fine," Abbey said politely,

which was true; she felt a resurgence of energy.

"You got any other kids in this town?" Scott asked.

"Are there any girls my age?" Susan added.

"My heavens, yes. We had twenty-five students last year. I'll have one of the boys introduce you around later, Scott." She turned her attention to Susan. "How old are you?"

"Seven."

Pearl's smile deepened. "I believe Chrissie Harris is seven. Her father works for the Parks Department and serves as our PSO on the side. PSO stands for public safety officer — sort of our policeman. Chrissie will be mighty glad to have a new friend."

"What about me?" Scott asked. "I'm nine."

"Ronny Gold's about that age. You'll meet him later. He's got a bike and likes to ride all over town on it, so there's no missing him."

Scott seemed appeased. "Are there any Indians around here?" he asked next.

"A few live in the area — Athabascans. You'll meet them sometime," Pearl assured him.

Looking around, Abbey felt a large mosquito land on her arm. She swatted it away. Susan had already received one bite and was swatting at another mosquito.

"I see you've been introduced to the Alaska state bird, the mosquito," Pearl said, then chuckled.

"They're pretty thick around here in June and July. A little bug spray works wonders."

"I'll get some later," Abbey said. She hadn't realized mosquitoes were such a problem in Alaska.

"Come on — let's go to the restaurant and I'll introduce you to Ben and the others," Pearl said, urging them across the road toward a building that resembled a house with a big porch. A huge pair of moose antlers adorned the front. "This is the Hard Luck Café. Ben Hamilton's the owner, and he's been cooking up a storm all day. I sure hope you're hungry."

Abbey grinned broadly. "I could eat a moose."

"Good," Pearl said, grinning back.

"I do believe it's on the menu."

Children.

Sawyer had no one to blame but himself for not knowing that Abbey came as a package deal. He was the person who'd so carefully drawn up the application. Obviously he'd forgotten to include one small but vital question. He'd left one little loophole. If Abbey had arrived with kids, would other women bring them, too? It was a question he didn't even want to consider.

Children.

He poured himself a mug of coffee from the office pot and took a swallow. It burned his mouth and throat, but he was too preoccupied to care. He had to figure out what they were going to do about Abbey Sutherland and her kids.

It wasn't that he objected to Scott and Susan. Abbey was right; her children had nothing to do with her ability to hold down the job of librarian. But they were complications the town hadn't foreseen.

First, the three of them couldn't live in that cabin. The entire space was no bigger than a large bedroom. Those cabins had never been intended as permanent living quarters, anyway. Sawyer remembered that initially he'd tried to reason with Christian and the others, but no one would listen, and he'd ended up taking the path of least resistance. He'd even helped clean the cabins!

In fact, he had to admit he'd become caught up with the idea himself. It had seemed like a simple solution to a complex problem. You'd think a group of men, all of whom were over thirty, would have the brains to know better.

Sawyer could only imagine what his older brother would say when he found out what they'd done. Charles would be spitting nails.

Sawyer passed his hand over his eyes and sighed deeply. He didn't understand what would bring a woman like Abbey Sutherland to Hard Luck in the first place. She wouldn't last, and he'd known it the moment he laid eyes on her.

It occurred to him that she might be running away. From her ex-husband? Perhaps she'd gotten involved in an abusive relationship. His hands formed tight fists at the thought of her husband mistreating her — at the thought of any man mistreating any woman.

Sawyer had seen for himself the dull pain in her eyes when she said she was divorced. He just wasn't sure why it was there. Understanding women wasn't his forte, and he felt himself at a real disadvantage. He lacked the experience, but he liked to think he was generally a good judge of character.

Then again, maybe he wasn't. There'd been only one serious relationship in his life, and that hadn't lasted long. Just when he was feeling comfortable with the way things were going, Loreen had started hinting at marriage. Soon those hints had become ultimatums. He'd liked Loreen just fine, but he wasn't anywhere close to marriage. Once he'd told her that, she left him.

Sawyer assumed that was how a lot of women felt. They wanted a ring to make everything official and complete. Well, he'd seen what could happen when a couple fell out of love. His parents were the perfect example of the kind of relationship he didn't want. They'd been chained to faded dreams and unhappy memories. So Sawyer had let Loreen go, and try as he might he hadn't once regretted his decision.

Sawyer didn't know how he was going to handle the problem of Abbey and her family. What he *should* do was put her and those two kids of hers on the afternoon flight out of Hard Luck.

But he wouldn't. Because if he even suggested it, twenty men would happily lynch him from the nearest tree. Of course, they'd have to go more than two hundred miles to find a tree tall enough for the job. . . .

After he finished his coffee, Sawyer headed over to the café. It seemed half the town was there, eager to meet Abbey. There was no place to sit, so he stood, arms folded and one foot braced against the wall, hoping to give the impression that he was relaxed and at ease.

Ben, he noted, was pleased as a pig in . . . mud to be doing such a brisk business. The cook wove his way between the mismatched tables, refilling coffee cups and making animated conversation.

He lifted the glass pot toward Sawyer with a questioning look.

Sawyer shook his head. He sure didn't need another coffee. In fact, he shouldn't have had the last one.

He saw that Abbey was surrounded by four of his pilots. They circled the table where she sat with Pearl and her children, like buzzards closing in on a fresh kill. You'd think they'd never seen a woman before.

His crew was a mangy-looking bunch, Sawyer mused, with the exception of Duke, who was broad-shouldered and firm-muscled. One thing he could say about all of them was that they were excellent pilots. Lazy SOBs when the mood struck them, though. He didn't know anyone who could love flying as much as a bush pilot and still come up with the world's most inventive excuses to avoid duty.

Everyone plied Abbey with questions. Sawyer half expected all this attention to fluster her, but she handled their inquisition with graceful ease. He was astonished by how quickly she'd picked up on names and matched them to faces.

Ben sauntered over to his side.

His gaze followed Sawyer's. "Pretty, isn't she?" Ben said. "I wouldn't mind marrying her myself."

"You're joking." Sawyer's eyes narrowed as he studied his long-time friend.

Ben's heavy shoulders shook with silent laughter. "So that's the way it is."

"Which way is that?" Sawyer challenged.

"She's already got you hooked. In no time, you'll be just like all the others, fighting for the pleasure of her company."

Sawyer snorted. "Don't be ridiculous! I just hope we don't have any more women arriving with families in tow."

Ben's mouth fell open. "You

didn't know about the kids?"

"Nope. Christian didn't, either, from what she said. Ms. Sutherland claims she didn't get a chance to tell him."

"Well, no one'll have a problem with a couple more kids in Hard Luck," Ben commented.

"That's not the point."

Ben frowned. "Then what is?"

"The cabins. Abbey can't live in one of those cabins with her children."

Ben leaned against the wall with Sawyer. "Yeah, you're right. So, what are you going to do?"

"No idea." Sawyer shrugged, trying to seem nonchalant. "It isn't like there's a house available for us to rent."

"Catherine Fletcher's place is vacant."

Sawyer shook his head. He wouldn't even consider approaching Catherine's family, and he doubted his brothers would be willing to do so either, regardless of the circumstances.

The bad blood between the two families ran deep. It would take a lot more than needing an empty house to wipe out forty years of ill will.

Catherine Harmon Fletcher was in poor health now, and in a nursing home in Anchorage, close to her daughter.

Ellen, Sawyer's mother, had suffered so much unhappiness because of Catherine. But she no longer lived in Hard Luck either. She'd remarried and had relocated to British Columbia, as happy as Sawyer had ever known her. He didn't begrudge his mother her new life. He figured she deserved it after all the miserable years she'd endured.

"What about Pearl's? She's going to be moving in with her daughter," Ben reminded him.

Sawyer hated to see the older woman go, but she'd told him it was time for her to move on, especially now that her friends had mostly left.

"Pearl's not leaving until we hire a replacement and she's had the opportunity to train her," Sawyer said.

Ben mulled over the problem for

several minutes. "What about the lodge?" he asked. "I know it's been years since anyone's stayed there, but —"

"The lodge?" Sawyer repeated. "You're joking!"

"It'd take a little work. . . ."

"A little work!" Sawyer knew he was beginning to sound like a parrot, repeating everything the other man said, but the idea was ludicrous. The lodge was in terrible shape. It would take months of hard work and thousands of dollars to make it livable. If it hadn't been so much trouble, they would have refurbished it, instead of dealing with the cabins. But those, at least, were in one piece.

A fire had burned part of the

lodge the year their father died, and not one of the three brothers had ever had the heart to get it repaired.

Their mother had always hated the lodge, which had become a symbol of everything that was wrong with her marriage, and she'd used the fire as an excuse to close it completely. If it'd been up to him, Sawyer would've torn the place down years ago. As it was now, the largest building in town stood vacant, a constant reminder of the father he'd loved and lost.

Ben wiped his forehead. "Yeah. The lodge wouldn't work. It's a shame, really."

Sawyer wasn't sure if Ben was talking about the abandoned lodge or Abbey's situation.

There was no easy solution. "I don't know what we're going to do," he muttered.

Ben was silent for quite some time, which was unusual for him. He studied Abbey and the children, then turned to Sawyer. "I guess you could send her back." His voice was carefully casual.

"I know."

"Is that what you plan to do?"

Sawyer felt a twinge of regret. "I can't see that we have any choice, do you?"

"It's a simple misunderstanding," Ben said. "No one's to blame. She should've told Christian about the kids."

The twinge had become an ache, and it didn't want to go away.

"Maybe Christian should've asked." But it didn't matter; she was here now, there was no place for her to live and *he* had to deal with it.

Better Abbey should return to Seattle immediately, Sawyer reasoned, before he found himself making excuses for her to stay.

CHAPTER 4

Sawyer knew he wouldn't be winning any popularity contests around Hard Luck if he announced that Abbey Sutherland and her children had to leave. The best way to handle the situation, he decided after giving it serious thought, was for Abbey to back out of the contract on her own — with a little help from him.

He waited until everyone had finished eating before he worked his way over to the table where she sat with Pearl. "I'll show you to your cabin now," he offered.

She looked up at him uncertainly, as if she wasn't quite sure of his motives. "I'd appreciate that."

"Sawyer," Pearl said, placing her hand on his forearm.

Sawyer already knew what the older woman was about to say. Like him, Pearl must have realized immediately that Abbey and her children couldn't live in a dilapidated old cabin outside town.

"When can I meet your dog?" Scott asked eagerly.

"Soon," Sawyer promised. Eagle Catcher didn't take easily to strangers; the husky wouldn't allow the boy to come near him until after two or three visits. Sawyer decided he'd bring Scott over to the house that evening and show him Eagle Catcher's pen. But the kid would be long gone before the husky accepted him as a friend.

"I'd like to see the library, too, if it wouldn't be too much trouble," Abbey said.

"Of course," Sawyer said in a friendly voice, but a shiver of guilt passed through him. When he'd last spoken to his mother, he'd told her they'd hired a librarian. Ellen had been excited to learn that her gift to the town was finally going to be put to use.

Sawyer squeezed the four of them into the cab of his pickup and drove down the main road. There were a couple of short side streets, but none that anyone had bothered to name.

"What's that?" Susan asked, pointing to a small wooden structure that stood outside the mercantile. She giggled. "It looks like a little house on stilts."

"It's called a cache. We use it to store food and keep it safe from bears and other marauding animals."

"Alaska's got lots of bears," Scott murmured as if he was well versed in the subject. "I read about them in the books Mom brought home from the library."

"How come the cache has legs that look like they're wearing silver stockings?" The question came from Susan again.

"That's tin," Sawyer explained, "and it's slippery. Discourages those who like to climb."

"I wouldn't try and climb it," Scott said.

"I don't think he's referring to boys," Abbey told her son. "He was talking about the animals."

"Oh."

"Is it still in use?" Abbey asked.

"Yes, it is. I don't know what Pete keeps in there during the summer months, but it's a crude kind of freezer in winter."

"I see."

"Oh, this is Main Street," Sawyer said as they continued down the dirt road. Dust scattered in every direction, creating a dense cloud in their wake.

"I wondered if there'd be any leftover snow," Abbey said. She seemed to be trying to make polite conversation.

"It hasn't been gone all that long." Sawyer knew he should use the opportunity to tell her how harsh the winters were and how bleak life was during December, January and February, but he was afraid Abbey would see straight through him. He preferred to be a *bit* more subtle in his attempt to convince her to go home.

"Is that the school?" Scott asked, pointing to the left.

"Yup."

"It sure is small."

"Yup. We've got two teachers. One for grades one through eight and another for high school. We had more than twenty students last year."

"Ben told me you've got a new elementary teacher coming soon," Abbey said.

"That's right." The state provided living quarters for the teacher. The house was one of the best in town, with all the modern conveniences. It was a palace compared to the cabin that would be Abbey's.

They drove past the lodge with its ugly black scars. Susan pressed her face to the window, and Sawyer waited for another barrage of questions, but none was forthcoming.

"Is the cabin close by?" Abbey asked. They'd already passed the outskirts of Hard Luck.

"Not much farther."

She glanced over her shoulder, as if gauging the distance between the town and her new home.

Sawyer parked in front of the cluster of small cabins and pointed to the one that had been readied for her. Seeing it now, battered by time and the elements, Sawyer experienced a definite feeling of guilt. The idea of luring women north with the promise of housing and land had been a bad idea from the first.

"*These* are the cabins your brother mentioned?" Abbey kept her voice low, but her shock was all too evident.

"Yes." This was the moment Sawyer had dreaded.

"We're supposed to *live* here?" Scott asked in the same incredulous tone.

"I'm afraid so."

Susan opened the truck door and climbed out. The seven-year-old planted her hands on her hips and exhaled loudly. "It's a dump."

Sawyer said nothing. Frankly, he agreed with the kid.

"It looks like one of those places where you freeze meat in the winter, only it isn't on stilts," Scott muttered.

Without a word Abbey walked into the cabin. Sawyer didn't follow; he knew what she was going to see. A single bed, a crude table and solitary chair, along with a woodstove. A small store of food supplies, stacked in a primitive cupboard.

"Mom," Scott wailed, "we can't live here!"

"It is a bit smaller than we expected," Abbey said. Her shoulders seemed to droop with the weight of her disappointment.

Hands still on her hips, Susan stood there, feet wide apart, as she surveyed the cabin. She shook her head. "This place is a dump," she repeated.

"Where's the bathroom?" Scott asked, giving the one-room interior a second look.

"There's an outhouse in the back," Sawyer told him. "Just take the path."

"What's an outhouse?" Susan

asked her mother.

Abbey closed her eyes briefly. "Follow Scott and you'll find out for yourself."

The two disappeared, and Abbey turned to Sawyer. He thought she'd yell at him, call him and his brother jerks for misleading her. Instead, she asked, "What about the twenty acres?"

"It's, uh, several miles to the east of here," he explained reluctantly. "I have the plot map in the office and I'll show you later if you want."

"You mean to say the cabin doesn't sit on the twenty acres?"

"No," he answered, swallowing hard. When they'd initially discussed the details of this arrangement, it had all seemed equitable.

Sort of. After all, Midnight Sons was picking up the women's airfare and related expenses. But at the defeated, angry look in Abbey's eyes, Sawyer felt like a jerk. Worse than a jerk. He wished she'd just yell at him.

"I see," she said after a long silence. Her voice was so low Sawyer had to strain to hear.

He clenched his hands into tight fists to keep from taking her by the shoulders and shaking some sense into her. Was she actually thinking of staying? Christian and the others were so starved for female companionship, they'd have promised the moon to induce women to move to Hard Luck. He didn't excuse himself; he'd played a major role in this deception, too.

"I found the outhouse," Susan said, holding her nose as she returned to her mother's side. "It stinks."

"What are we gonna do?" Scott asked, sounding desperate.

"Well," Abbey said thoughtfully, "we'll have to move a pair of bunk beds in here and add a couple of chairs."

"But, Mom . . ."

Sawyer glanced inside the cabin and groaned inwardly.

"We'll make it a game," Abbey told her children with forced enthusiasm. "Like pioneers."

"I don't wanna play," Susan whined.

"Maybe there's someplace else we

can rent," Scott said, looking hopefully at Sawyer.

"There isn't." He hated to disappoint the boy, but he couldn't make houses that didn't exist appear out of the blue. He turned to Abbey, who continued to stare impassively in the direction of the cabin. He suspected she was struggling to compose herself.

"Could you show me the library now?" she finally asked. Apparently she wanted to see the whole picture before she decided. Fair enough. Sawyer hoped that once she'd had time to analyze the situation, she'd make a reasonable decision. The *only* reasonable decision.

They all piled back into the truck. On the drive out to the cabin all three Sutherlands had been filled with anticipation. The drive back was silent, their unhappiness almost palpable.

The urge to suggest that Abbey give up and leave was almost more than Sawyer could suppress. But he'd be tipping his hand if he so much as hinted she fly home. He'd say something eventually if need be, but he'd rather she reached that conclusion herself.

The log building designated for the library had once belonged to Sawyer's grandfather. Adam O'Halloran had settled in the area in the early 1930s. He'd come seeking gold, but instead of finding his fortune, he'd founded a community.

Since the day they'd heard that Christian had hired a librarian, Sawyer and the other pilots had hauled over a hundred or more boxes of books from Ellen's house, which was now Christian's.

The original O'Halloran home consisted of three large rooms. Abbey walked inside, and once more her disappointment was evident. "I'll need bookshelves," she said stiffly. "You can't store books in boxes."

"There are several in Mother's house. I'll see that they're delivered first thing tomorrow morning."

Her gaze shot to his. "Is your mother's house vacant?"

Sawyer knew what she was thinking. He shook his head. "Mom's remarried and out of the state, but Christian lives there now. Although he's away at the moment, as you know."

"I see."

A young boy who introduced himself as Ronny Gold walked his bicycle up to the door and peeked inside. Scott and Ronny stared at each other.

"Can you play?" Ronny asked.

"Mom, can I go outside?"

Abbey nodded. "Don't be gone long." She glanced at her watch. "Meet me back here in half an hour, okay?"

"Okay." Both Scott and Susan disappeared with Ronny.

Hands buried deep in his pants pockets, Sawyer watched as Abbey

174

lifted a book, studied the spine, then picked up another. She handled each one with gentle reverence.

Sawyer waited until he couldn't bear it any longer. He'd planned to give her more time to realize she couldn't possibly live under these conditions. But if she wasn't going to admit it herself . . .

"It isn't going to work, Abbey," he said quietly. "It was a rotten idea, bringing women to Hard Luck. I blame myself. I should never have agreed to this."

"You want me to leave, don't you?" she asked in an ominously even voice, ignoring his comment.

Sawyer didn't answer. He couldn't, because he refused to lie or mislead her any further. What surprised him most was his own realization — that he'd have liked the opportunity to know her better. Instead, he was forced to send her back to Seattle, where she and her children belonged.

He steeled himself. He and Christian weren't the only ones at fault.

"You misled my brother," he said gruffly and couldn't decide who he was angriest with. Christian? Abbey? Himself?

"*I* misled Christian?" Abbey cried, her voice bordering on hysteria. "I find that insulting."

The anger that had simmered just below the surface flared to life. "You duped him into hiring you without once mentioning that you had children!" Sawyer snapped. "I know there was nothing on the application about a family." That was one problem he was going to correct at the first opportunity. "But you should've been more honest, since you were aware that we offered housing as part of the employment package."

"*I* should've been more honest? That's the height of hypocrisy! I was told I'd be given living quarters and twenty acres of land, but you neglected to tell me the cabin's the size of a doghouse." She dragged in a deep breath. "How dare you suggest I broke the agreement? I'm here, aren't I?"

"You broke the spirit of our agreement."

"Oh, please! As for your free land, that's a big joke, too. You forgot to mention that it's so far from town I'd need a dogsled to reach it. If you want to talk about someone breaking the agreement, then let's discuss what you and your brother have done to me and my children."

At the pain in her eyes, he felt worse than ever. He had no defense, and he knew it. "All right. We made a mistake, but I'm willing to pay your airfare home. It's the least we can do."

"I'm staying," she said flatly. "I signed a contract, and I intend to hold up my end of the bargain, despite . . . despite everything."

Sawyer couldn't believe his ears. "You can't!"

Her eyes flashed. "Why can't I?"

"You saw the cabin yourself. There's no way the three of you could possibly live there, bunk beds or not. You might be able to manage this summer, but it'd be out of the question once winter sets in."

"The children and I are staying." She said this with such determination Sawyer could readily see that nothing he said or did would change her mind.

"Fine," he said brusquely. "If that's your decision." At best, he figured she'd last the night. By morning she'd be at the airfield with her luggage, anxious to catch the first plane out of Hard Luck.

An hour later Abbey sat on the

edge of the thin mattress and tried to think. She hadn't felt so close to tears since the day she'd filed for divorce. In some ways, the situation felt very similar to the end of her marriage. She was being forced to admit she'd made a mistake. Another in what seemed to be a very long list.

It hadn't felt like a mistake when she'd accepted the job. It had felt decidedly right.

The problem was that she didn't want to leave Hard Luck. She'd painted a fairy-tale picture of the town in her mind, and when it fell short of her expectations she'd floundered in disappointment. Well, she'd been disappointed before and learned from the experience. She would again.

No matter how eager Sawyer O'Halloran was to be rid of her, she was staying.

Really, she had no one to blame but herself. Her father had told her the free cabin and twenty acres sounded too good to be true. She was willing to concede that he was right. But it wasn't just the promise of a home and land that had drawn her north.

She'd come seeking a slower pace of life, hoping to settle in a community of which she'd be a vital part. A community where she'd know and trust her neighbors. And, of course, the opportunity to set up and manage a library was a dream come true. She'd moved to

Hard Luck because she realized being here would make a difference. To herself, to the town, to her children most of all. She'd come so Scott and Susan would only read about drive-by shootings, gang violence and drug problems.

Although her children's reactions to the cabin had been very much like her own, Abbey was proud of how quickly the two had rebounded.

"It isn't so bad here," Scott had told her when he'd returned to the O'Halloran homestead with Ronny Gold. Susan had met Chrissie Harris and they'd quickly become fast friends.

The sound of an approaching truck propelled her off the bed in a near panic. She wasn't ready for another round with Sawyer O'Halloran!

Sawyer leapt out of the cab as if he wanted to spend as little time as possible in her company. "Your luggage arrived." Two suitcases were on the ground before she reached the truck bed. Pride demanded that she get the others down herself. He didn't give her a chance.

Despite the ridiculous accusations he'd made, despite his generally disagreeable nature, Abbey liked Sawyer. She'd seen the regretful look in his eyes when he'd shown her the cabin. It might be fanciful thinking on her part, but she believed he'd wanted her to stay. He might not think it was practical or smart, but she sensed that he wanted her here. In Hard Luck.

He might provoke her, irritate her, accuse her of absurd things; yet she found herself wishing she could get to know him better.

That wasn't likely. Sawyer O'Halloran had made his views plain enough. For whatever reasons, he wanted her gone.

All the suitcases were on the ground, but Sawyer lingered. He started to leave, then turned back.

"I shouldn't have said that, about you duping Christian. It wasn't true."

"Are you apologizing?"

He didn't hesitate. "Yes."

"Then I accept." She held out her hand.

184

His fingers closed firmly over hers. "You don't have to stay in Hard Luck, Abbey," he said. "No one's going to think less of you if you leave."

She held her breath until her chest began to ache. "You don't understand. I can't go back now."

Frowning, he released her hand. "Why can't you?"

"I sold my car to pay for the kids' airfare."

"I already told you I'd buy your tickets home."

"It's more than that."

He hopped onto the tailgate and she joined him. "I want to help you, if you'll let me," he said.

She debated admitting how deeply committed she was to this

venture, then figured she might as well, because he'd learn the truth sooner or later.

"My furniture and everything I own is in the back of some truck on its way to Alaska. It should get here within a month."

He shook his head. "It won't, you know."

"But that's what I was told!"

"Your things will be delivered to Fairbanks. There's no road to Hard Luck."

She wasn't completely stupid, no matter what he thought. "I asked Christian and he told me there's a haul road."

"The haul road is only passable in winter. It's twenty-six miles to the Dalton Highway, which doesn't even resemble the highways you know. It's little more than a dirt and gravel road. A haul road's much worse. It crosses two rivers and they need to freeze before you can drive over them."

"Oh."

"I'm sorry, Abbey, but your furniture won't go any farther than Fairbanks."

She took this latest bit of information with a resigned grimace. "Then I'll wait until winter. It's not like I have any place to put a love seat, do I?" she asked, gesturing at the cabin.

"No, I guess you don't." He eased himself off the tailgate, then gave her a hand down. "I need to get back to the airfield."

"Thanks for bringing our luggage."

"No problem."

"Mom. Mom." Scott came racing toward her. Keeping pace with him was a large husky. "I found a dog! Look." He fell to his knees and enthusiastically wrapped his arms around the dog's neck. "I wonder who he belongs to."

"That's Eagle Catcher," Sawyer said as his eyes widened in shock. "My dog. What's he doing here? He should be locked in his pen!"

That evening, Sawyer sat in front of a gentle fire, a book propped in his hands. Eagle Catcher rested on the braided rug by the fireplace. The book didn't hold his attention.

He doubted that anything could distract him from Abbey and her two children.

In all the years he'd lived in Hard Luck, Sawyer had only known intense fear once, and that had been the day his father died.

He never worried, but he did this June night. He worried that Susan or Scott might encounter a bear on their way to the outhouse. He worried that they'd face any number of unforeseen dangers.

He couldn't help recalling that Emily O'Halloran, an aunt he'd never known, had been lost on the tundra at the age of five. She'd been playing outside his grandparents' cabin one minute and was gone the next. Without a sound.

Without a trace.

For years his grandmother had been distraught and inconsolable over the loss of her youngest child and only daughter. In fact, Anna O'Halloran had named the town. She'd called it Hard Luck because of her husband's failure to find the rich vein of gold he'd been looking for; with the tragedy of Emily's death, the name took on new significance.

Worrying about Abbey and her children was enough to ruin Sawyer's evening. Surely by morning she'd see reason and decide to return to Seattle!

Eagle Catcher rose and walked over to Sawyer's chair. He placed his head on his master's knee.

"You surprised me, boy," Sawyer said, scratching his dog's ears. He wouldn't have believed it if he hadn't seen it with his own eyes. Eagle Catcher and Scott had acted as if they'd been raised together. The rapport between them had been strong and immediate. The first shock had been that the dog had escaped his pen and followed Sawyer's truck; the second, that he'd so quickly accepted the boy.

"You like Scott, don't you?"

Eagle Catcher whined as if he understood and was responding to the question.

"You don't need to explain anything to me, boy. I feel the same way." About Abbey. About her children.

He tensed. The only solution was for Abbey to leave — for more reasons than he wanted to think about. He prayed she'd use common sense and hightail it out of Hard Luck come morning.

The cabin wasn't so bad, Abbey decided after her first two days. It was a lot like camping, only inside. She could almost pretend it was fun, but she longed for a real shower and a meal that wasn't limited to sandwiches.

Other than their complaints about having to use an outhouse, her children had adjusted surprisingly well.

The summer months would be tolerable, Abbey thought, but she couldn't ignore Sawyer's warning about the winter.

As for her work at the library, Abbey loved it. Sawyer had seen to the delivery of the bookcases from his mother's house, along with a solid wood desk and chair for her.

The day after her arrival, Abbey had set about categorizing the books and creating a filing system. Someday she planned to have everything on a computer, but first things first.

"How are things going?" Pearl Inman asked, letting herself into the library.

"Fine, thanks."

"I brought you a cup of coffee. I was hoping to talk you into taking a short break."

Abbey stood and stretched, placing her hands at the small of her back. "I could use one." She walked to the door and looked outside, wondering about Scott and Susan, who were out exploring. It was all so different from their life in a Seattle highrise. She knew Scott and Ronny spent a good part of each day down at the airfield pestering Sawyer.

If Scott wasn't with Ronny, then he was with Sawyer's dog. Abbey couldn't remember a time her son had been so content.

Susan and Chrissie Harris spent nearly every minute they could with each other. In two days' time they'd become virtually inseparable. Mitch Harris had stopped by to introduce himself. Mitch, Abbey recalled, worked for the Department of the Interior and was the local public safety officer. He seemed grateful that his daughter had a new friend.

"I can't believe the progress you've made," Pearl said, surveying the room. "This is grand, just grand. Ellen will be delighted."

Abbey knew that Ellen was Sawyer's mother and the woman who'd donated the books to the town.

"I don't suppose you've seen Sawyer lately?" Pearl asked, pouring them each a cup from her thermos.

"Not a word in almost two days," Abbey admitted, hoping none of her disappointment showed in her voice.

"He's been in a bad mood from the moment you got here. I don't know what's wrong with that boy. I haven't seen him behave like this since his father died. He blamed himself, you know."

Abbey settled on a corner of the desk and left the chair for the older woman.

"What happened to his father?"

Pearl raised the cup to her lips. "David was killed in an accident several years ago. They'd flown to one of the lakes for some fishing, which David loved. On the trip home, the plane developed engine trouble and they were forced down. David was badly injured in the crash. It was just the two of them deep in the bush." She paused and sipped at her coffee.

"You can imagine how Sawyer must have felt, fighting to keep his father alive until help arrived. They were alone for two hours before anyone could reach them, but it was too late by then. David was gone."

Abbey closed her eyes as she thought of the stark terror that must have gripped Sawyer, alone in the bush with his dying father.

"If I live another sixty years I'll never forget the sight of Sawyer carrying his father from the airfield. He was covered in David's blood and refused to let him go. It was far too late, of course. David was already dead. We had to pry him out of Sawyer's arms."

"It wasn't his fault," Abbey whispered. "It was an accident. There was nothing he could've done."

"There isn't a one of us who didn't tell him that. The accident changed him. It changed Hard Luck. Soon Ellen moved away and eventually remarried. Catherine Fletcher grieved something fierce. That was when her health started to fail."

"Have I met Catherine?" Abbey asked, wondering why Pearl would mention a woman other than David's wife.

"Catherine Fletcher. Used to be Catherine Harmon. No . . . no, she's in a nursing home in Anchorage now. Her daughter lives there."

Pearl must have read the question in Abbey's eyes. "Catherine and David were engaged before World War II. She loved him as a teenager and she never stopped. Not even when she married someone else. David broke her heart when he returned from the war with an English bride."

"Oh, dear."

"Ellen never quite fit in with the folks in Hard Luck. She seemed different from us, standoffish. I don't think she meant to be, and I don't think she realized how she looked to others. It took me a few years myself to see that it was just Ellen's way. She was really quite shy, felt out of place. It didn't help any that she didn't have children right away. She tried. God knows she wanted a family. They were married almost fifteen years before Charles was born."

"You said Catherine got married?" Abbey asked, her heart aching for the jilted woman.

"Oh, yes, on the rebound, right after David returned from the war. She gave birth to Kate nine months later and was divorced from Willie Fletcher within two years."

"She never remarried?"

"Never. I thought for a time that she and David would get back together, but it wasn't to be. Ellen left him, you see, and returned to England. Christian was about ten at the time. She was gone well over a year." She shook her head, then

200

sighed. "You can understand how David's death affected everyone in town. Especially Sawyer."

"Of course."

"What I don't get is why he's upset now. He's walking around like a bear with a sore paw, snapping at everyone."

Abbey gaped at her. "You think it's got something to do with me?"

"That's my guess. But what do I know?" Pearl asked. She drank the rest of her coffee and stood up to leave. "I'd best get back to the clinic before someone misses me." The clinic was in the community building, close to the school and the church.

She tucked the thermos under her arm. "So, are you staying in Hard

Luck or not?" she asked. Her question had an edge to it, as if she wasn't sure she was going to like the answer.

Abbey told her the truth. "I'd like to stay."

"That doesn't answer my question."

Abbey grinned. "I'm staying."

Pearl's lined face softened. "Good. I'm glad to hear it. We need you, and I have a feeling Sawyer wants you to stay, too."

Abbey laughed in disbelief. "I doubt that." And if it was true once, she felt certain it no longer was.

"No, really," Pearl countered. "Unfortunately that boy doesn't have the brains of a muskrat when it comes to dealing with an attractive woman." She made her way to the door. "Give him time and a little patience, and he'll come around." With a cheerful wave, Pearl left.

Abbey returned to work and got busy unloading another box of Ellen's books. Knowing what she did now, the collection took on new meaning for her. Many of the books dated from the early to mid-fifties. Those were the childless years, when Ellen had yearned for a baby. Abbey suspected that Ellen O'Halloran had gained solace from these books, that they'd substituted for the friends she hadn't been able to make in this town so far from England.

As she set a pile of Mary Roberts Rinehart mysteries on the desk, she heard the distinctive sound of Sawyer's truck pulling up outside.

Her heart started to race, but she continued working.

He stormed inside and stood in the doorway, hands on his hips. His presence filled the room until Abbey felt hedged in by the sheer strength of it. "Have you decided to stay?" he demanded.

"Yes," she answered smoothly. "I'm staying."

"You're sure?"

"Yes," she said with conviction. And she *was* sure. During her conversation with Pearl, she'd made up her mind.

"Fine. You're moving."

"Where?" Abbey had been told often enough that there wasn't any other place available.

"You can stay in Christian's house. He phoned this afternoon, and he's decided to make a vacation out of this trip. I'll let him decide what to do with you when he gets home."

CHAPTER 5

"What?" Abbey's eyes flashed with annoyance — and confusion. "I'm not moving into your brother's home."

The last thing Sawyer had expected was an argument. Okay, so maybe he hadn't made the offer as graciously as he should have, but he had an excuse.

The woman was driving him crazy.

Worrying about her and those two kids stuck out on the edge of town had left him nearly sleepless for two nights. It wouldn't have bothered him as much if there'd been neighbors close at hand. But so far, the other cabins remained empty.

"You won't be there long," he said. And he'd thought he was doing her a favor! He should've known that nothing with Abbey would be easy.

She picked up another of his mother's books, handling it with respect, then added the author and title to a list. "The kids and I are doing well where we are. Really."

"There are dangers you don't know about."

"We're fine, Sawyer."

He inhaled sharply. "Why won't you move?"

Abbey's shoulders lifted in a small, impatient sigh. "It isn't *entirely* your brother's fault that he didn't know about Scott and Susan."

"True, but you aren't entirely to blame either."

"It's very thoughtful of you to offer me the house, but no thanks." She glanced up and gave him a quick smile. For a second Sawyer swore his heart was out of control, and all because of one little smile.

"All right," he said, slowly releasing his breath, "you can move into my house, then, and I'll stay at Christian's."

"Sawyer, you're missing the point. I don't want to put anyone out of his home."

"Christian isn't there to put out."

"I know that, but when he does return I'll have to go back to the cabin. There's nowhere else for me and the children to move. I can't see that shuffling us from one temporary place to another is going to help."

"But —"

"We're better off making do with what we have," she said, cutting off his argument.

"Are you always this stubborn?"

Abbey's eyes widened as if his question surprised her. "I didn't realize I was being stubborn. It doesn't make sense to play musical houses when we have a perfectly good — When we have a home now."

"The cabins were never intended to be full-time residences," he said, clenching his fists at his sides. He shouldn't admit it, especially since his brother had begun interviewing job applicants again, promising them free housing and land. Sawyer hadn't wanted him to do it, but Christian had gotten carried away. You'd think that with the Seattle press picking up on the story, Christian would reconsider his approach. At least — thank God — the reporters had stopped calling *him.* And nothing Sawyer could say seemed to dampen his brother's enthusiasm for the project. Christian was having the time of his life.

Well, when the next women started to show up, Sawyer decided, he'd let Christian escort them to those shacks and gleefully announce that here were their new homes. No way was he going to do it.

"I don't want you to think I'm being unappreciative," Abbey said.

"You're being unappreciative," he muttered. "Christian's place has all the conveniences. Surely the kids miss television."

"They don't." She hesitated and bit her lip. "Though I'll confess I'd like a . . . hot shower."

Sawyer could tell that she was tempted by the offer.

"I'm not comfortable knowing you're out on the edge of town alone," he told her. "Because of the kids . . . People in town would be mighty upset if something happened. Pearl's been at me to find you some other place to live." He didn't want her to think there was anything *personal* in his concern. "Anyway, Christian'll be gone a month or more."

"A month," Abbey repeated.

"Perhaps we could compromise," he said, walking forward and supporting his hands on her desk. "You could move into Christian's house or mine, whichever you decide, until one of the other women arrives. Then perhaps you could share the place until a more viable solution presents itself." Her hair smelled of wildflowers, and he found himself struggling to keep his mind on business.

"When's the next woman flying in?"

"I'm not sure. Soon."

She took a moment to consider, then thrust out her hand. "Thank you. I accept your offer."

Relieved, Sawyer shook her hand as briefly as possible without being rude. The softness of her skin, her scent, her combination of vulnerability and fierce determination — it was all too attractive. Too disruptive. His world, so orderly and serene before her arrival, felt as if it had been turned inside out.

One thing was sure — he didn't like it.

"I'll stop by later and pick up your luggage," he said.

Her eyes moved to meet his, and

she gave him another of those heart-tripping smiles. There was something so genuine and unself-conscious about it. Their eyes held a moment longer, and every muscle in his body was telling him to lean forward and kiss her. As soon as the impulse entered his mind, he sent it flying. The last thing he wanted was to become involved with Abbey Sutherland.

"Mom —" Scott burst into the room like a warlord roaring into battle "— can I have lunch at Ronny's? His mom said it's okay."

Sawyer leapt back so fast he practically fell over Eagle Catcher, who'd ambled into the room with Scott.

"Hi, Mr. O'Halloran," the boy

said in a near squeak, then stared down at the husky. His face flushed with guilt.

Sawyer looked from the dog to the boy. "How'd Eagle Catcher get out of his pen?"

Scott lowered his head.

"Scott, did you let him out of his pen?" Abbey asked.

His nod was barely perceptible. "I went to visit him and he whined and whined, and I was going to put him back, honest I was."

Sawyer crouched down so he could speak to Scott at eye level. "I know you and Eagle Catcher are good friends, and I think that's great."

"You do?" Scott's eyes rounded with surprise.

"But it's important that you ask my permission before you let him out of his yard. Otherwise, I could come home and not know where he is."

"I went to visit him, but he didn't want me to leave," Scott explained. "Every time I started to go, he'd cry. I only opened the gate so I could pet him and talk to him. I must not have latched it very good, because he followed me."

"Next time make sure the latch is secure," Abbey told him sternly.

Scott's gaze avoided Sawyer's. "I might not have closed the gate all the way on purpose."

Sawyer tried to hide his amusement. "Thank you for being honest about it. Next time you want to play with my dog, all you have to do is come and ask me first. That won't be difficult, will it?"

"No, sir, I can do that."

"Good."

"Eagle Catcher only likes *me,* you know," Scott announced proudly. "He wouldn't leave the pen for Susan or Ronny." He closed his mouth when he realized what he'd admitted.

So the three friends had been in his yard and attempted to lure Eagle Catcher out of the fenced-off area.

"So, can I have lunch at Ronny's?" Scott asked again, obviously eager to change the subject.

"All right, but I want you to take Eagle Catcher back to his pen.

Later on you and I are going to have a long talk about Mr. O'Halloran's dog."

"Okay," he said sheepishly, and before she could say another word, he dashed out the door, the husky at his heels.

Sawyer chuckled. "I can't believe the way those two hit it off. It's not like Eagle Catcher to become this attached to someone."

"I hope this doesn't develop into a problem," Abbey said. "He's got to understand that it's your dog, and he has to obey your rules. But Scott's always loved dogs, especially huskies, and we've never been able to have one. He was crazy about Eagle Catcher from the first time he saw him."

"The feeling appears to be mutual. Eagle Catcher's never had anyone lavish attention on him the way Scott does. They seem destined for each other, don't they?"

Abruptly Abbey looked away.

Sawyer wondered what he'd said that had caused such a startled reaction. Did she think he was talking about the two of *them*? If so, Abbey Sutherland was in for a surprise.

Sawyer wasn't interested in marriage. Ever. Not even to the beautiful Abbey Sutherland. He'd learned all the lessons he needed from his own experience several years before. And from his parents, who'd tried to make their marriage work, but only made each other miserable. Sawyer wanted none of that.

Rarely had Abbey enjoyed a shower more. She stood under the warm spray as it pelted against her skin and savored each refreshing drop.

Exhausted from a day of playing, Scott and Susan fell asleep the minute they climbed into the two single beds in Christian O'Halloran's guest bedroom.

Abbey was sleeping in the double bed in a second spare bedroom. Although Sawyer had repeatedly told her she was welcome in his brother's home, Abbey couldn't shake the feeling that she was invading Christian's privacy.

It was fine for Sawyer to offer his brother's house. But Abbey couldn't help wondering if he'd bothered to mention it to Christian.

After she toweled off, she dressed in jeans and a thin sweater and walked barefoot to the kitchen, where she made herself a cup of tea. It was difficult not to compare her stark living quarters at the cabin and the simple luxuries of Christian's home.

The kitchen was large and cheery, the white walls stenciled with a blue tulip pattern. The room's warmth and straightforward charm reminded her that Ellen O'Halloran had once lived here. Her touch was evident throughout the house.

Taking her tea with her, Abbey

wandered onto the front porch and sat in the old-fashioned swing. Mosquitoes buzzed about until she remembered to light the citronella candle. The evening was beautiful beyond anything she'd imagined. Birds chirped vigorously in the background. The tundra seemed vibrant with life.

Although it was nearly ten, the sky was as bright as it had been at noon. Cupping the mug in her hands, she looked past the small patch of lawn to Sawyer's house across the street.

His home clearly lacked a woman's influence. He, too, had a yard, but there were no flower boxes decorating the window ledges, no beds blooming with hardy perennials. The porch was smaller, almost as if it had been added as an afterthought.

Drawing her knees up under her chin, Abbey gazed unseeingly at the house while she reviewed her situation. She'd taken the biggest gamble of her life by moving to Hard Luck. No one had told her she was playing against a stacked deck. But the stakes were too high for her to back down now. She wouldn't. Couldn't. Somehow, she'd find the means to stay and make a good life for herself and her children.

The front door of Sawyer's house opened, and he stepped onto the front porch. He leaned against the support beam, holding a mug in his hands. For what seemed a long time, they did nothing but stare at each other.

As if he'd reached some sort of decision, Sawyer set the mug aside and crossed the street. "Do you mind if I join you?" he asked.

"Not at all." Abbey hoped she didn't sound as shy as she felt. She slid over so there was plenty of room on the swing.

"My mother used to sit out here in the summer," Sawyer reminisced. "There were many nights I'd get ready for bed and I'd look out and see her sitting exactly where you are, swinging as if she was eighteen again and waiting for a beau."

A sadness crept into his voice, and

from the little she knew about his parents' marriage, she guessed his perception could be right. His mother might well have been waiting for the man she loved to join her — the husband she'd once, and perhaps still, loved.

He seemed to have read her thoughts. "My parents didn't have a good marriage. Don't get me wrong — they rarely raised their voices to each other. In some ways I wish they had. It might have cleared the air. Instead, they practiced indifference toward each other." He hesitated and shook his head. "I don't know why I'm telling you all that. What about your parents?"

"They're great. They've had their

share of squabbles over the years and still argue now and then. But underneath it, well, all I know is that they're deeply committed to each other." She paused, thinking about the fact that they'd disagreed with her move to Hard Luck. "My family gave me a firm foundation, and for that I couldn't be more grateful." She wondered how the conversation had become so personal. "I particularly appreciated that foundation when my marriage fell apart.

"My parents were wonderful. They'd never liked Dick, but they'd raised me to make my own choices and gave me the freedom to learn from my mistakes without I-told-you-so lectures." Abbey stopped, a little flustered. She hadn't meant to discuss her marriage, especially with someone she barely knew.

"Does your ex have contact with Scott and Susan?"

"No. And he hasn't paid a penny of support since he left the army. I haven't seen him in years, and neither have the kids. In the beginning I had a lot of anger. Not so much because of the money — that isn't nearly as important as everything else. Then I realized it's Dick's loss. He's the one who's missing out on knowing two fabulous kids, and now I just feel sorry for him."

Sawyer reached for her hand and she held his tightly as tears clouded her eyes. She looked away, hoping he wouldn't notice.

"Abbey, I'm sorry. I didn't mean to pry."

"You didn't. I don't know what's wrong with me. I don't usually tear up like this."

"Maybe it's because you're a long way from home."

"Are you going to start that again — telling me I should go back to Seattle?" The argument had grown tiresome.

He didn't answer for a moment. "No." His free hand touched her cheek and brushed a tendril of hair aside. Their eyes met in a rush of discovery. It seemed inevitable that he'd kiss her.

It had been a long time since she'd been kissed. An even longer time since she'd wanted a man to kiss her this much. Sawyer lowered his mouth to hers and she leaned forward shyly.

As soon as Sawyer's mouth touched hers, she experienced a re-awakening. She felt . . . cherished. For years she'd been the protector, standing alone against the world, caring for her children. She hadn't had either time or energy to think of herself as feminine and desirable. Sawyer made her feel both.

She opened her lips to him, and an onslaught of need stole her breath. She felt as though she'd taken a free-fall from twenty thousand feet.

Sawyer eased his mouth from hers, then brought it back as if he needed a second kiss to confirm what had happened the first time. His tenderness produced an overwhelming ache deep inside her. One that was emotional, as well as physical. Those feelings had been so long repressed she had trouble identifying them.

Sawyer lifted his mouth from Abbey's. Slowly she opened her eyes and found him studying her. His eyes were intense with questions.

She smiled, and at the simple movement of her lips he groaned and leaned forward, kissing her with a passion that left her breathless and weak.

Whatever happened to her in Hard Luck, whatever became of

the housing situation, whatever took place between her and Sawyer from this point onward, Abbey knew that in these moments, they'd shared something wonderful. Something special.

He ended the kiss with reluctance. Abbey hid her face in his shoulder and took one deep breath after another.

They didn't speak. She sensed that words would have destroyed the magic. He gently rubbed her back.

"I'd better go home," he whispered after a while.

She nodded. He loosened his hold, then released her. Abbey watched as he stood, buried his hands in his pockets . . . and hesitated.

He seemed about to speak, but if that was the case, he changed his mind. A moment later, he whispered a good-night and walked across the street to his own home.

Abbey had the distinct feeling that they wouldn't discuss this evening. The next time they met it would be as if nothing had happened between them.

But it had. . . .

After an hour of restlessly pacing the floor, Sawyer sat down at his desk and leafed through his personal phone directory. He needed to talk to Christian, the sooner the better.

He called Directory Assistance to

get the number of Christian's hotel in Seattle — or, at least, his last-known residence there. Christian might not even *be* in Seattle anymore — but Sawyer swore he'd find him if it took the rest of the night.

He waited for the hotel operator to answer. As luck would have it, Christian was still registered at the Emerald City Empress. The operator connected him with his room.

Christian answered on the fourth ring, sounding groggy.

"It's Sawyer."

"What time is it?"

"Eleven."

"No, it isn't." Sawyer could visualize his brother picking up his watch and staring at it. "It might be eleven in Hard Luck, but it's midnight here. What's so important that it can't wait until morning?"

"You haven't called me in days."

"You got my message, didn't you?"

Sawyer frowned. He had; that was what had prompted him to move Abbey into Christian's house. "Yeah, I got it. So you're taking some personal time."

"Yeah. Mix business with pleasure. I might as well, don't you think?"

"*You* might think of phoning more often."

Christian groaned. "You mean to say you woke me up because we haven't talked recently? You sound like a wife checking up on her husband!"

"We've got problems." Sawyer gritted his teeth.

"What kind of problems?"

"Abbey Sutherland's here."

"What's the matter? Don't you like her?"

Sawyer almost wished that was true. Instead, he liked her too much. He liked her so much he'd completely lost the ability to sleep through an entire night. Either he was pacing the floor, worried about her living in that cabin alone with her two children, or he was fighting the instinct to walk across the street and make love to her. Either way, he was fast becoming a lunatic.

"I like her fine. That's not the problem."

"Well, what is?"

"Abbey didn't arrive alone." A short silence followed his announcement. "She brought her two children."

"Now, just a minute," Christian said hurriedly. If he wasn't awake earlier, he was now. "She didn't say a word about having any children."

"Did you ask?"

"No . . . but that shouldn't have mattered. She might have said something herself, don't you agree?"

"All I know is we'd better revise the application. Immediately."

"I'll see to it first thing in the morning." His promise was followed by the sound of a breath slowly being released. "Where's she staying? You didn't stick her in one of the cabins, did you? There's barely room for one, let alone three."

"She insisted that was exactly where she'd stay — until I convinced her to move into your house."

"My house!" Christian exploded. "Thanks a lot."

"Can you think of anyplace else she could live?"

There was a moment's silence. "No."

"I tried to talk her into moving back to Seattle, but she's stubborn." And beautiful. And generous. And so much more . . .

"What are we going to do with her once I return?" Christian asked.

237

"Haven't got a clue."

"You're the one who told me to hire her," his brother argued.

"I did?"

"Sure, don't you remember? I was telling you about Allison Reynolds and I mentioned there were two women I was considering for the position of librarian. You said I should hire the one who wanted the job."

So apparently Sawyer was responsible for his own misery.

"Maybe she'll fall in love with John or Ralph," Christian said hopefully, as if this would solve everything. "If she gets married, she won't be our problem. Whoever's fool enough to take her on — *and* her children — will be responsible for her."

Anger slammed through Sawyer, and he had to struggle to keep from saying something he'd later regret.

"Any man who married Abbey Sutherland would be damn lucky to have her," he said fiercely.

"Aha!" Christian's laugh was triumphant. "So that's the way it is!"

"How much longer do you plan to be in Seattle?" Sawyer asked, ignoring his brother's comment. A comment that was doubly irritating because it echoed one made by Ben the very day of Abbey's arrival.

"I don't know," Christian muttered. "I've been busy interviewing women, and I'd like to hire a couple more. I haven't even gotten around to ordering the supplies and plane parts. While I'm here, I thought I'd take a side trip up to see Mom. She'd be disappointed if I didn't."

"Fine, go see Mom."

"By the way, Allison Reynolds decided she wanted the position, after all. Take my advice, big brother, and don't get all excited over this librarian until you meet our new secretary," Christian said. "One look at her'll knock your socks off."

"What about a health-care specialist?"

"I've talked to a few nurses, but nothing yet. Give me time."

"Time!" Sawyer snapped. "It isn't supposed to take this long."

"What's your hurry?" Christian asked, and then chuckled. An evil sound, Sawyer thought sourly. "The longer I'm gone, the closer your librarian friend will be." Laughter echoed on the line. "I love it. You were against the idea from the beginning — and now look at you."

"I'm still against it."

"But not nearly as much as you were *before* you met Abbey Sutherland. Isn't that right?"

Abbey stood in front of the lone store in town, popularly known as the mercantile. It was decorated in a style she was coming to think of as Alaskan Bush — a pair of moose antlers adorned the doorway. She walked inside with a list of things she needed. The supplies she'd been given when she got to Hard

Luck were gone. She also craved some fresh produce, but was afraid to find out what that would cost.

A bell over the door jangled, announcing her arrival.

The mercantile was smaller than the food mart where she bought gas back in Seattle. The entire grocery consisted of three narrow aisles and a couple of upright freezers with price lists posted on the door. A glass counter in front of the antique cash register displayed candy and both Inupiat and Athabascan craft items.

A middle-aged man with a gray beard and long hair tied back in a ponytail stepped out from behind the curtain. He smiled happily when he saw her. "Abbey Sutherland, right?"

"Right. Have we met?"

"Only in passing." He held out his hand for her to shake. "I'm Pete Livengood. I own the store and I have a little tourist business on the side."

"Pleased to meet you," she said, smiling back, wondering how much tourist trade he got in Hard Luck. "I want to pick up a few things for dinner this evening."

"Great. Let me have a look at your list and I'll see what I can do."

Abbey watched as he scanned the sheet of paper. "We don't sell fresh vegetables here since most folks have their own summer gardens. Every now and then Sawyer brings me back something from Fairbanks, but it's rare. Wintertime's a different story, though."

"I see." Abbey had hoped to serve taco salad that evening. She knew the kids would be disappointed.

"Louise Gold's got plenty of lettuce in her garden. She was bragging about it just the other day. I suspect she'd be delighted if you'd take some of it off her hands."

"I couldn't ask her." Abbey had only met Ronny's mother briefly. The Gold family had been very kind, and she didn't want to impose on their generosity any more than she already had.

"Things are different in the Arctic," Pete explained. "Folks help one another. If Louise knew you wanted lettuce for your dinner and she had more than she needed, why, she'd be insulted if you didn't ask. Most folks order their food supplies a year at a time. I'll give you an order form. Louise can probably help you with it better than I can, since you're buying for a family of three."

"A *year* at a time?"

"It's more economical that way."

"Oh."

"Don't worry about this list. I know how hard you're working setting up the library. I'll take care of everything you have here myself, including talking to Louise about that lettuce."

"Oh, but . . . I couldn't ask you to do that."

"Of course you could. I'm just being neighborly. Tell you what. I'll get everything together and deliver it this afternoon. How's that?"

"Wonderful. Thank you."

"My pleasure," Pete said, grinning broadly as if she'd done him a favor by allowing him to bring her groceries.

As the day went on, Abbey found herself waiting for Sawyer, hoping he'd stop by, wondering if he'd mention their kisses. Knowing he wouldn't.

Scott and Susan were in and out of the library all morning. Abbey enjoyed being accessible to her children; the experience of having them close at hand during the summer was a new one.

When she'd asked Pearl about

day care, the older woman had thought she was joking. There was no such thing in Hard Luck. Not technically. Abbey knew that Louise Gold watched Chrissie Harris for Mitch, but there wasn't any official summer program for school-age children.

Scott and Susan were thriving on the sense of adventure and freedom. Their happiness seemed to bubble over.

"Hi, Mom," Scott said, strolling into the library, Eagle Catcher beside him.

"Once the library opens, we can't have Sawyer's dog inside," she told him.

"We can't?" Scott was offended on the husky's behalf. "That's not fair. I let him come everyplace else I go."

"Dogs can't read," she said, raising her eyebrows.

"I bet I could teach him."

She shook her head. "Did you ask Sawyer about letting him out of his pen?"

"Yup. I went down to the airfield. He was real busy, and I thought he might get mad at me, but he didn't. He said I'd been patient and he was proud of me." Scott beamed as he reported the compliment. "He's short-handed 'cause his brother's gone, and he had to take a flight this morning himself. I don't think he wanted to go, but he did."

"Oh." She tried to conceal her disappointment. "Did he say when he'd be back?"

"Nope, but I invited him for dinner. That was okay, wasn't it?"

"Ah . . ."

"You said we were having taco salad, didn't you?"

"Yes . . . What did Sawyer say?"

"He said he'd like that, but he wanted to make sure you knew about him coming. I told him you always fix lots, and I promised to tell you. It's all right, isn't it?"

Abbey nodded. "I suppose."

"I'll go see if Sawyer's back yet. I'll tell him you said he could come." Scott raced out the door at breakneck speed, with Eagle Catcher in hot pursuit. Abbey couldn't help grinning — it took the energy of a sled dog to keep up with her son.

She was barely aware of the afternoon slipping past until Pete Livengood stopped by with her groceries and surprised her with a small bouquet of wildflowers. His thoughtfulness touched her.

Abbey was straightening everything for the day when a shadow fell across her desk. She looked up to find Sawyer standing in the doorway, blocking the light.

He seemed tired and disgruntled. "Isn't it about time you went home?"

"I was just getting ready to leave."

"Scott invited me to dinner."

"So I heard." She found herself staring at him, then felt embarrassed and looked away. Her thoughts were in a muddle as she scrambled for something to say to ease the sudden tension between them.

"Pete Livengood brought me wildflowers," she blurted, convinced she sounded closer to Susan's age than her own.

"Pete was here?"

"Yes, he delivered a few groceries. He's a very nice man."

Sawyer was oddly silent, and Abbey tried to fill the awkward gap.

"When he stopped by, we talked for a bit. He's led an interesting life, hasn't he?"

"I guess so." Sawyer frowned. "Do you have any idea how old Pete Livengood is?" he demanded.

"No." Nor did she care. In fact,

she couldn't think of a reason it should matter. He was a rough-and-ready sort who'd lived in Alaska for close to twenty years. Abbey found his stories interesting and had asked him questions about his life. Perhaps Sawyer objected to her spending so much time away from her job.

"Pete's old enough to be your father!"

"Yes," she said curiously. "Is that significant?"

Sawyer didn't respond. "I gave specific instructions that you weren't to be bothered."

"Pete didn't bother me."

"Well, he bothers me," Sawyer said abruptly.

"Why?"

Sawyer expelled his breath and glanced up at the ceiling. "Because I'm a fool, that's why."

CHAPTER 6

The atmosphere in the Hard Luck Café was decidedly cool when Sawyer came by for breakfast.

"Morning," he greeted Ben, then claimed a seat at the counter. Three of his pilots were there, and he nodded in their direction. They ignored him.

Ben poured him a cup of coffee.

"I'll take a couple of eggs and a stack of hotcakes." Sawyer ordered without looking at the menu.

John Henderson grumbled something Sawyer couldn't hear, slapped some money down on the counter and walked out. Ralph, who sat two stools down from Sawyer, followed suit. Duke muttered a few words, then he was gone, too.

Sawyer looked up, surprised. Three of his best pilots acted like they couldn't get away from him fast enough. "What? Do I have bad breath?"

Ben chuckled. "Maybe, but that ain't it."

"Why are they mad at me?"

Ben braced his hands on the counter. "I'd say it has something to do with Abbey Sutherland."

Sawyer tensed. "What about Abbey?"

"From what I hear, you had a

word with Pete Livengood about him dropping off Abbey's groceries at the library."

"Yeah? So what?" To Sawyer's way of thinking, the old coot had no business interrupting her when she was at work. The library wasn't open yet. Besides, Pete hadn't brought that bouquet of wildflowers because he was interested in finding a good book to read. No, he was after Abbey. That infuriated Sawyer every time he thought about it.

Pete wasn't right for Abbey, and Sawyer wasn't planning to let him pester her while she was on his property. Okay, so maybe his family *had* donated his grandfather's cabin to the town. It didn't matter;

Sawyer felt responsible for her. If it wasn't for Midnight Sons, she wouldn't even be in town.

"Just remember I'm a disinterested observer," Ben said. "But I've got eyes and ears, and I hear what the men are saying."

"So what's the problem?"

Ben brought the eggs and cakes hot off the griddle, and topped up Sawyer's coffee. "Ralph and John and a couple of the others object to you keeping Abbey to yourself."

Sawyer didn't see it that way. "What gives them the idea I'm doing that?"

"Wasn't it you who warned everyone to stay away from the library?"

"That isn't because I'm keeping Abbey to myself," he argued. "The

257

woman's got work to do, and I don't want her constantly interrupted."

"I sure don't remember you taking such a keen interest in your mother's collection before."

Sawyer wasn't going to argue further, although the whole discussion irked him. No one seemed to appreciate what he was trying to do. "The library will be open soon, and then the men can visit as often as they like."

That seemed to appease Ben, and Sawyer suspected it would appease the other men, as well.

"Next on the list of complaints," Ben continued, "the guys think you're inventing flights to keep the crew busy so you can court Abbey without interference."

"I'm not *courting* her," he said heatedly. "And what kind of old-fashioned word is that anyway?"

"You had dinner at her house, didn't you?"

"That's true, but Scott was the one who invited me." He hated having to defend his actions. That aside, it was the best dinner he'd had all summer. And he didn't just mean the food.

"Are you saying you don't have any personal interest in her?"

"That's right." Although he didn't hesitate, Sawyer wondered how honest he was being. It was a good thing no one knew he'd been kissing Abbey.

Ben narrowed his eyes. "You're

not interested in her," he repeated. "Is that why you nearly bit Pete's head off?"

Sawyer sighed, his appetite gone. "Who told you that? I didn't so much as raise my voice."

"But you made it clear you didn't want him seeing her."

"Not before the library's open," Sawyer insisted. "This is the very reason I was against the idea of recruiting women in the first place. Look at us!"

"What?" Ben asked.

"A few weeks ago we were all friends. Don't you see what's happening? We're at each other's throats."

"Well, we got one thing settled, though, didn't we? You're not interested in her yourself."

"Of course not," Sawyer said stiffly.

"Then you won't mind if a few of the other guys develop intellectual interests that require research trips to the library?"

Sawyer shrugged. "Why should I care?"

"That's what I'd like to know," Ben said, and Sawyer had a feeling the old stew-burner was seeing straight through him.

"All I ask is that the guys give Abbey a little breathing room. Can't they wait until the library's open?"

"And when will that be?"

"Soon," he promised. "I understand she'll be ready to open it up to the public in a few days."

"Good. I'll pass the word along," Ben said, then returned to the kitchen.

Sawyer ate his breakfast, and although Ben was an excellent cook, the food rested in his stomach like a lead weight.

It didn't take him long to acknowledge that he was guilty of everything Ben had suggested. He'd gone out of his way to keep the men as far from Abbey as he could arrange. It hadn't been a conscious decision, at least not in the beginning. But it was now.

Abbey was putting away the last of the dinner dishes the following night when she heard Scott and

Susan on the front porch talking with a third person. The weather had been warm, and she'd changed into shorts when she got home from work. Who'd have believed it would reach the mid-eighties in the Arctic? Despite everything she'd read, it hadn't seemed real until she'd experienced it for herself.

Drying her hands on a kitchen towel, she walked out to the porch to discover Sawyer chatting with her children. Eagle Catcher stood at his side.

"Hello," he said cheerfully when she joined them.

"Good evening." She'd been hoping she'd see Sawyer again soon. His eyes said he was eager for her company, too.

Being with him felt right. She loved the easy way he spoke to her children, his patience with Scott over the dog, his gentleness with Susan. Her daughter had adored him from the moment he'd held out his hand to her when they'd met at the airport.

"When are we going to see the northern lights?" Scott asked Sawyer. He'd talked of little else over dinner that night. "Ronny told me it's better than the Fourth of July fireworks, but no matter how late I try to stay up, it won't get dark."

"That's because it's early summer, Scott, and the solstice isn't even due for another two weeks. Wait until the end of August — you'll probably begin to see them then."

"Does it *ever* get dark in Alaska?" Susan asked.

"Yes, but just for a short time in the summer. Winter, however, is another story."

"Ronny told me it's dark practically all day," Scott put in, "but I knew that from the books Mom read when she applied for the job."

"What do the northern lights look like?" Susan asked.

Sawyer sat on the swing and Susan sat beside him; Scott hunkered down next to Eagle Catcher. "Sometimes the light fills the sky from horizon to horizon. It's usually milky green in color and the colors dance and flicker. Some folks claim they can hear them."

"Can you?"

Sawyer nodded. "Yup."

"What's it sound like?"

Sawyer's eyes caught Abbey's. "Like tinkling bells. I suspect you'll hear them yourself."

"Are they always green?"

"No, there's a red aurora that's the most magnificent of all."

"Wow, I bet that's pretty!"

"You know, the Inuit have a legend about the aurora borealis. They believe the lights are flaming torches carried by departed souls who guide travelers to the afterlife."

Abbey sat on the edge of the swing. Soon Susan was in her lap, and she was next to Sawyer. He looked over at her and smiled.

Her children seemed to have a hundred questions for him. He told them the story of how his grandfather had come to Hard Luck, chasing a dream, searching for gold.

"Did he find gold?" Scott asked.

"In a manner of speaking, but not the gold he'd been looking for. It was here, but he never really struck it rich. He died believing he'd failed his wife and family, but he hadn't."

"Why did he stay?" Abbey asked.

"My grandmother refused to go. They had a little girl named Emily who disappeared on the tundra, and afterward my grandmother wouldn't leave Hard Luck."

"Did she think there was some

chance Emily would come back?"

"She never stopped looking."

"What do you think happened to her?" Scott asked.

"We can only guess, but none of the prospects are pleasant. That's why it's so important for you never to wander off on your own. Understand?"

The two children nodded solemnly.

Abbey glanced at her watch, surprised by how late it was. When she'd read that Alaska was the land of the midnight sun, she'd assumed the light would be more like dusk. She was wrong. The sun was so bright she had to prop a board against the curtains in the children's bedroom to make it dark enough for them to fall asleep. As it was, their routines had started to shift. They stayed awake later and slept in longer.

"Bedtime," she told them now.

Her announcement was followed by the usual chorus of moans and complaints.

"Come on, Susan," Sawyer said, standing. "I'll give you a piggyback ride." He hoisted her onto his back and Susan giggled, placing her arms around his neck.

"You're next, partner," he told Scott.

"I'm too old for that stuff," Scott protested, but Abbey knew it was for show. He was as eager as his sister for a ride.

"Too old? You've got to be kidding," Sawyer said, his voice rising in exaggerated disbelief. "You're never too old for fun." Then, before Scott could escape, Sawyer clasped him around the waist and held him against his side.

Scott was giggling and kicking wildly. With a smile, Abbey held open the screen door, and Sawyer carried the children down the hallway to the bedroom they grudgingly shared.

"How about a cup of coffee?" she asked while the kids changed into their pajamas. "Or I could make tea."

His eyes brightened momentarily, then he shrugged and shook his head. "I can't. Thanks, anyway. I came over to tell you I talked to my brother about the housing situation."

Susan burst out of the bedroom wearing her Minnie Mouse pajamas and ran into the kitchen. Scott was close behind, his pajama top half over his head. When her kids were this excited, it was always a while before they settled down enough to sleep.

"Will you tuck me in?" Susan asked, gazing up at Sawyer.

He glanced at Abbey. "If it's okay with your mother."

They hopped up and down as if it were Christmas morning and they'd awakened to find the tree surrounded by gifts.

Taking him by the hand, Susan led Sawyer into the bedroom. Abbey followed, her arm around Scott's shoulders. Sawyer tucked each child into bed, but it was soon apparent that neither one intended to go to sleep.

"Tell us a story," Susan pleaded, wriggling out from under the covers. She hugged her favorite doll.

Scott, too, seemed to think this was a brilliant idea. "Yeah!" he shouted. "One with a dog in it." It went without saying that he would've welcomed Eagle Catcher in his bedroom had Abbey and Sawyer allowed it.

"All right," Sawyer agreed. "But then you have to promise to close your eyes and go to sleep."

Sawyer entertained them with a story for the next fifteen minutes.

He was obviously inventing as he went along, and Abbey was both charmed by his spontaneity and moved by his willingness to do this for her children. Afterward, emotion tugged at her heart as Sawyer bowed his head while each child recited a prayer.

A few minutes later, he slipped out of the bedroom. Abbey was waiting for him in the kitchen. She was boiling water for a cup of tea.

"Thank you," she whispered, not looking at him.

There was an uncomfortable silence, then Sawyer cleared his throat. "As I said, I spoke with Christian about the housing situation. It's clear to both of us that you and the children can't go back to the cabin."

"But I don't really have any choice, do I?"

"There's one vacant house in town." His lips thinned. "It belongs to Catherine Fletcher."

The name was vaguely familiar, and Abbey tried to recall where she'd heard it. Then she remembered the day Pearl Inman had stopped by the library and told her about Sawyer and his family, and some of Hard Luck's history. If she recalled correctly, the two families had been at odds since the 1940s right after World War II.

"Christian thought we should contact Catherine's family. She's in a nursing home now, and it's unlikely she'll ever return to Hard

Luck."

"I'd be happy to pay whatever rent she feels is fair."

"Midnight Sons will pick up the rent," Sawyer said. "We promised you free housing when you agreed to move here, and that's what you're going to get."

"Do you think she'll let me have the house?" Abbey asked hopefully.

Sawyer frowned. "She's a cantankerous old woman, and it'd be just like her to refuse out of spite. I'm hoping I don't have to speak to her at all. Her daughter's far more reasonable."

"You don't like Catherine?"

"No," Sawyer said without emotion. "She went out of her way to hurt my mother, and I don't find that easy to forgive. It's a long story better left untold."

Despite his negative feelings toward the old woman, Sawyer was willing to approach her on Abbey's and the children's behalf. Every day Abbey found a new reason to be grateful for Sawyer's presence in her life.

"I appreciate what you're doing," she murmured. "Are you sure you don't have time for a cup of coffee or tea?"

His eyes held hers, and a warm sensation skittered through her. Hastily he shook his head. "I've got to get back." He looked past her down the hallway that led to the bedrooms. "You were right when you said your husband was the one to be pitied. Scott and Susan are great kids. They'd make any man proud."

He moved past her, then paused on his way out the door and kissed her. Only their lips touched. The kiss was brief and casual, as if they exchanged such an intimacy every day.

It didn't strike Abbey as unusual until he'd left the house. One hand covering her mouth, she watched him from the screen door.

His steps seemed to have an un-characteristic bounce. He was half-way across the narrow dirt road when he appeared to realize what he'd done. He stopped abruptly and whirled around.

"Good night, Sawyer," she called.

He raised his hand in farewell, then continued across the street to his own home.

"Midnight Sons," Sawyer barked into the receiver, stretching the phone cord as far as it would go so he could reach a pad of paper.

"Sawyer, it's Christian. Listen up. Allison Reynolds is on her way."

Sawyer blinked. "Who?"

There was a loud, exasperated sigh. "Our new secretary. I talked to her this morning, and she's back from vacation and ready to start work first thing Monday morning."

"Great. This is the woman who doesn't type, right?"

"She won't need to. Besides, there's more to being a secretary than typing. Don't worry, what she lacks in one area she makes up for in others."

That didn't warrant a comment. "Have you booked her flight?" he asked.

"Yeah. She's coming in on Friday morning. Same flight Abbey Sutherland did."

Sawyer wrote down the information. "I'll send Duke in to meet her," he said. That should quell some of the dissension among the men.

"Not Duke," Christian protested. "Send Ralph."

"Why not Duke?"

"He'll talk her head off, and you know what a chauvinist he can be. I don't want Allison's first impression to be negative."

"Fine. I'll send Ralph."

"Ralph," Christian repeated the pilot's name slowly. "No, maybe John would be better," he suggested.

John? It was his big mouth that scared off the last teacher! "Why not Ralph?"

"He's too eager, you know? He might say something that would offend Allison."

"Why don't you get your butt home so you can pick her up yourself?" It seemed to Sawyer that his brother was being *much* too particular.

"I would if I could get there in time. I've interviewed a nurse I think would be excellent. I know you asked me to wait on hiring anyone else, but this gal is perfect."

"Then do it." If she met the qualifications, Sawyer couldn't understand the problem.

"She's older. Way older. Pete Livengood's age."

"So?" All the better as far as Sawyer was concerned. Then maybe Pete would stop showing interest in Abbey.

"I was hoping to find someone younger. Attracting women to Alaska isn't as easy as it sounds. I get plenty of calls, but once they hear exactly how *far* north we are, they start asking a lot of questions." He paused. "I had to do some fast talking to convince Allison to give us a try."

"Every position can't be filled with Allison clones," Sawyer said testily.

"I know. I know. Listen, I'll talk to you again soon. I'll want to know how Allison's adjusting."

"Fine."

"Any word from Charles lately?"

"None, but I expect he'll show up any day, hungrier than a bear and meaner than a wolverine." Their eldest brother kept his own hours. He was often gone for weeks at a time, then would blow into town with his geological equipment and stay for a month or two. There was a restlessness in Charles that never seemed to ease. Sawyer didn't question it, but he didn't understand it, either.

He spoke to his younger brother for a few more minutes. Sawyer hung up the phone to find John Henderson standing on the other side of the desk.

"You got a minute?" the pilot asked nervously.

Sawyer nodded. "Sure. What's the problem?"

"Not a problem as such. It's more of a . . . concern."

"Sit down." Sawyer motioned toward the vacant chair.

"If you don't mind, I prefer to stand," the other man said stiffly.

Sawyer arched his eyebrows and leaned back in his chair. "Suit yourself."

John folded his hands. He seemed to need a couple of minutes to gather his thoughts. Finally he blurted, "Me and a few of the other guys aren't happy with the way things are going around here."

"What things?"

Once more it appeared that John was having difficulty speaking his mind. "You've got an unfair advantage, and it's causing hard feelings."

Now Sawyer understood. After his talk with Ben, he should've realized sooner that this discussion wasn't about Midnight Sons at all. John had come to talk to him about Abbey.

"You're upset because I asked you not to disturb the new librarian while she organizes the library."

"Yes," he said angrily. "You ordered us to stay away until the library's open, but I notice the same doesn't apply to you."

"I'm her contact person," Sawyer explained, keeping his voice calm and even. "She needs someone who can help her, answer questions and so on."

"Let *me* be her contact person," John argued. "Or Duke. None of us would pester her. We just want to drop by the library and make her feel welcome. Everyone knows what happened when Pete went to see her. It wasn't right that you chewed him out for doing his job."

"Pete delivers groceries now? That's news to me."

"Come on, Sawyer, get real. If Abbey stopped by here and needed something, wouldn't you be willing to take it to her?"

Before Sawyer could respond, John continued.

"Of course you would. She's pretty and she's nice, and heck, I thought when we came up with the idea of bringing women to Hard Luck, we'd at least get to talk to them now and then."

Sawyer released a lengthy sigh. "Perhaps I have been a bit . . . overprotective."

Henderson's jaw tightened. "The guys are saying you want her for yourself."

Sawyer opened his mouth to disagree, then realized they had more than enough evidence to hang him. "You could have a point there."

"That's what we think. All we're asking is that you drop the restrictions on the rest of us. It's only fair. You have my word of honor that I won't bother her, and the others won't, either."

Sawyer couldn't see any choice. If he didn't do it, he'd have a mutiny on his hands. "Fine," he said reluctantly.

John relaxed. "No hard feelings?"

"None," Sawyer assured him. He picked his notepad and peeled off the flight information Christian had given him. "In fact, we've got another woman due to land on Friday. Would you be willing to pick her up?"

"Would I?" John's face broke into a wide grin not unlike the expression on Scott's face when Sawyer had given him permission to play with Eagle Catcher.

The pilot quickly composed himself. "I'll have to check my schedule."

"Do that and get back to me."

Abbey had no idea what was happening. She'd had four visitors in the past hour. Each had produced a valid reason for coming to the library. She hadn't realized how eagerly awaited the opening of the library was. In light of such overwhelming interest, she decided to do just that the next morning.

Abbey finished for the day and collected her things. She'd been visited by everyone but the one person she was aching to see.

As she walked toward Christian's house, she recognized the familiar sound of Sawyer's pickup behind her. She turned and waved.

He slowed to a crawl. "Heading home?"

"Yeah."

"How about a ride?"

She laughed. "It's less than two blocks."

Sawyer leaned over and opened the passenger door. "I thought I'd take the scenic route. Where are Scott and Susan?"

"In the yard. They wanted to run through the sprinkler." The temperature was in the low eighties for the second day in a row, and the kids loved it.

"Grab your swimsuit and a towel, and I'll take you and the kids to my favorite swimming hole," Sawyer suggested.

Abbey brightened. "You're on."

Scott and Susan came racing toward the truck when Sawyer pulled up.

"Hey, kids, want to go swimming?"

"Can Eagle Catcher come, too?"

"Sure. Hop in the back," Sawyer told them. "I'll just run and get my swimming trunks."

As he did that, Abbey hurried into the house and slipped out of her clothes and into her bathing suit. She almost hadn't packed it with the move. She threw on some shorts and a T-shirt, then grabbed towels and clothes for the children.

Sawyer drove out to the airfield and loaded them into a plane. He explained that this type had pontoons so it could land on the water. It was a tight squeeze with kids and dog, but they managed. The kids thought it was great fun.

"How far is this swimming hole of yours?" Abbey asked once they'd taxied off the runway and were in the air.

"Far enough for the kids to appreciate it when we get there."

From the air, there seemed to be a huge number of lakes. She did remember reading that there were — how many lakes? A lot — in Alaska, but knowing a geographical fact sure hadn't prepared her for actually seeing it. Above the noise of the engine, Sawyer told them he was taking them to an all-around favorite spot of his. Not only was the swimming great, the fishing was good, too.

It must have been an hour, perhaps longer, before Abbey noticed they were descending. She cast an anxious look at Sawyer before the plane glided gracefully onto the smooth water.

Once the engines had slowed, Sawyer steered the aircraft toward shore.

"Does anyone know we're here?" she asked.

"I left a note for Duke."

"But —"

"Trust me," he said. "I wouldn't

take Scott and Susan anywhere they wouldn't be perfectly safe." He patted her hand. "You, too."

"The kids have only had a few swimming lessons, but they're not afraid of the water." The lake was so clear Abbey could see the bottom. Near the shore, where Sawyer stopped, it appeared to be just three or four feet deep.

Various shrubs grew along the shoreline. Abbey recognized wild rose bushes and knew that in a month or so they'd be crowded with small, vibrantly pink flowers. It was easy to imagine the beauty they'd add to this already beautiful scene.

The minute they could step out of the plane, Scott and Susan were splashing about in the shallows. "It's cold, Mom!" Scott grinned at her, his teeth chattering. "Wow, and does it ever feel good!"

"It's lovely," she agreed, dipping in one foot. "What's the name of the lake, Sawyer?" She was thinking she'd look for it on a map when they returned to town.

Sawyer shrugged. "There are three million lakes in Alaska. They don't all have names. Let's call it . . . Abbey Lake."

"Abbey Lake!" Susan laughed.

"I like it," Abbey said, playing along. "It has a nice ring."

"Can we go in deeper now?" Scott asked. "I wanna swim."

"Hold your horses," Sawyer told him, tugging his shirt out of his waistband. He was undressed and down to his swimming trunks in almost no time; it took Abbey a little longer. Soon Sawyer and the two children were in waist-deep water and Scott and Susan were taking turns swimming short distances.

Abbey sat on the edge of the pontoon and dangled her feet in the water. It felt cold, but wonderfully invigorating.

"Come on, Mom! The water's great once you get used to it," Scott assured her.

"I think she might need some help getting wet," Sawyer teased.

"No . . . no! I'm fine." She saw the first splash coming in enough time to cover her face. But her defenses were hopeless against the concerted efforts of the other three. Within seconds she was drenched. "All right, you guys, this is war. The men against the women."

For a short while, pandemonium reigned. Abbey and Susan might have done more damage if they hadn't been laughing so hard. Abbey stumbled out of the water and onto the shore.

A few minutes later, Sawyer joined her. He wiped his wet face with his forearm, then sat next to her on the sun-warmed sand. He kept his gaze trained on the children, who continued to wage war and fun.

"This was a fantastic idea," she said, wringing out her hair. "Thank you for thinking of us."

"I've been doing a lot of that recently," he said in a low voice. "Thinking of you," he clarified. "I feel my brother and I misled you about Hard Luck."

"I was the one who made the decision to come. I knew what I was getting into. It's true the housing situation is a problem, but at the time you didn't know about the children."

"I wanted you to leave when you first came."

"I know," she said unevenly. His determination to be rid of her still rankled.

He glanced at her, his eyes intense. "I don't feel that way anymore."

"I'm glad," she whispered, finding it hard to keep the emotion out of her voice. She sighed, thinking how fortunate she was to have met Sawyer. He was wonderful with her children — wonderful with her. *To* her.

He looked away abruptly, as if the conversation had grown more personal than he'd intended. "When will the library open?"

"Funny you should ask. I had several inquiries this afternoon. I thought I'd place an Open sign on the door first thing in the morning."

"Terrific," he said, but it seemed to her that his response lacked enthusiasm.

Scott trotted out of the water and

stood before them.

With some relief, Abbey turned her attention to her son.

"I was just watching you," he said, directing the comment to Sawyer, "and it looked like you wanted to kiss my mother." He grinned, scrubbing water from his eyes with both hands. "You can if you want to," he announced, then raced back into the lake.

CHAPTER 7

At nine o'clock the following morning Abbey printed a huge Open sign and posted it outside the library. It wasn't long before her first customer arrived.

At five past nine, John Henderson ambled in, hands in his pockets. He was tall and husky, his boyish good looks set off by a thatch of honey-colored hair.

"Good morning," she said in a friendly tone.

"Mornin'," he returned almost

shyly. "Nice day, isn't it?"

"Sure is," Abbey agreed. The weather was unseasonably warm this year, she'd been told.

John wandered around the library scanning the rows of books. Everything was cataloged and carefully arranged — fiction in alphabetical order, nonfiction according to subject and children's books. She hoped to order some new titles soon.

"Is there anything I can help you find?" Abbey asked, eager to be of assistance.

"Yup."

"What do you like to read?"

"Romances," John said.

His choice surprised her, but she didn't let it show. Romances were generally considered women's fiction, but that didn't mean a man couldn't enjoy them.

"I need something that'll teach me how to tell a woman she looks even prettier than a shiny new Cessna."

"I see." She suspected it would take more than a romance novel to help him in that area.

"I want to be able to tell her how pretty I think she is, and how nice, but I need to know the right way to say it without riling her. Whenever I try to talk to a woman, all I seem to do is make her mad. Last time I tried, I didn't do so well."

Abbey walked over to the bookshelves and pretended to survey several titles while she thought over the situation.

"It's important that I learn how to talk to a certain woman right," John continued, " 'cause another man's got a head start on the rest of us." His voice tightened. "But that's not important now, all things being equal, if you know what I mean."

Abbey didn't, but feared an explanation would only confuse her further. "You might look down this row," she finally advised, directing him to books on etiquette and social behavior.

"Thanks," John said, grinning widely.

Abbey returned to her desk. No sooner had she sat down when Ralph Ferris, another of Sawyer's pilots, strolled in. He paused when he saw John. The two men glared at each other.

"What are you doing here?" Ralph demanded.

"What does it look like?"

"I've never seen you read a book before!"

"Well, I can start, can't I?" John glanced nervously at Abbey. "I have as much right to be here as you."

"Is there something I can help you find?" Abbey asked the new man.

"I see you shaved," Ralph taunted under his breath. He held his nose. "What kind of aftershave did you use? It smells worse than skunk cabbage."

"I borrowed yours," John muttered.

The two men engaged in a staring match, then each attempted to force the other away from the shelves. Bemused, Abbey watched Ralph ram his shoulder against John's. She saw John retaliate, jabbing the point of his elbow into Ralph's side. "Excuse me. If you two are going to fight, I'd prefer you didn't do it in the library," she admonished in her sternest librarian's voice.

The men scowled at each other, then rushed to stand in front of her desk. John spoke first. "Abbey, would it be all right if I stopped by at your house this evening?"

"How about dinner?" Ralph said quickly before she could answer.

"Ben's cooking up one of his specials — caribou Stroganoff."

"Dinner?" Abbey repeated, not knowing what to say.

Before she could respond, Pete Livengood marched in. His hair was dampened down as if he'd just stepped out of the shower. He carried a heart-shaped box.

"Chocolates," the two pilots said together. They sounded furious — and chagrined — as if they'd been outmaneuvered.

"Women like that sort of thing," Abbey heard one whisper to the other.

"Where are we going to get chocolates?" John murmured.

"I've got an extra can of bug spray," Ralph said. "Do you think she might like that?"

It was turning into one of the most unproductive days Sawyer had ever spent.

His men had invented one excuse after another to delay their routine flights. He didn't need anyone to tell him they'd gone to the library, and they weren't interested in checking out books, either.

Sawyer found himself increasingly impatient and ill-tempered. He refused to ask any of the men, but his curiosity made him incapable of concentrating. What was happening at that library? And how was Abbey reacting to all this attention? The prospect of her being with someone else drove him crazy.

Restlessly he stood in front of the office's only mirror, wondering if he should shave off his beard. He'd never asked Abbey how she felt about it. Although he'd worn a beard for more than ten years, he'd be willing to remove it if she asked.

He ran a hand along his face, then returned to his desk, slouching in the seat.

John had come back from the library first, clutching an old edition of Emily Post and a couple of paperback romances. Sawyer found him intently reading one of the love stories during his coffee break. He watched as John scanned a page or two, then set the book aside and stared into space, apparently mulling over some important matter.

Ralph had gone to the library that morning, too. He'd returned sporting a book on the history of aircraft, which he proudly showed to Sawyer.

"I understand another woman's coming in this week," Ralph said, lingering inside the office. He glared at John accusingly.

"That's right," Sawyer answered absently, reading over a flight schedule before handing it to Ralph.

"I'd like to ride along."

"You already have a flight on Friday."

Ralph lifted one shoulder in a shrug. "Duke'll take it for me. He owes me one."

Sawyer didn't hesitate long. If two

of the most woman-hungry of his men were vying for Allison Reynolds, maybe they'd leave Abbey alone. So he agreed — with one stipulation. Duke had to willingly consent to the change in plans. Sawyer refused to arbitrate in a conflict over this, he told Ralph, and he didn't want to hear another word about it. The other man's face fell as he walked out of the office and toward the airfield.

The day dragged by, with every pilot somehow managing to visit the library. The minute Sawyer was free, he hurried there himself. He knew something was wrong the minute he stepped inside.

Abbey sat at her desk reading, and when the door opened, she raised her head. Eyes narrowed, she slapped the book shut. After observing the loving way she'd handled the books earlier, that action surprised him.

"Good afternoon," he said warmly.

No smile. No greeting.

He missed the way her eyes lit up whenever they met. He missed her smile.

He tried again. "How's your day going?"

Silence.

"Is, uh, something wrong?"

"Tell me," she said in tones as cold as a glacier, "exactly why was I hired?"

"Why were you hired?" he repeated slowly, not understanding

her anger, let alone her question. "Hard Luck needed a librarian to organize a lending library."

"And that was the *only* reason?"

"Yes."

"Oh, really?" she spat out, her eyes blazing.

"Abbey, what's wrong?"

She stormed to her feet and folded her arms. The fire in her eyes was hot enough to scorch him from ten feet away. "All your talk about me breaking the spirit of the agreement! I can't believe I fell for that. You had me thinking you were upset because I hadn't told you about Scott and Susan. Well, everything's clear to me now."

"That's settled and done with. No one blamed you — it was as much our fault for not asking."

Abbey shook her head, but Sawyer wasn't sure what she meant. It did seem to him, though, that she was close to tears. He stepped toward her, but stopped short of taking her in his arms.

"Stay away from me."

"Abbey, please —"

"It wasn't a librarian you wanted," she said. "You and your men were looking for —" she paused as if she didn't know how to continue "— entertainment."

"Entertainment?"

"I don't know how I could've been so *stupid*. The ad practically came right out and said it. Lonely men! You weren't interested in my library skills, were you? No wonder everyone was so upset when I showed up with children."

"That's not true," he flared. He did value her professional skills — and he didn't want her dating *or* "entertaining" any other man. Today, with every unattached male in Hard Luck visiting the library, had made that very obvious.

"If the men in town are so lonely, why didn't you just advertise for wives?"

"Wives? We wanted women, but we didn't want to have to marry them."

Abbey's mouth fell open. "Oh. That makes it all right, then."

"We offered you a house and land, remember."

"In exchange for what?"

His temper was rising. "Not what you seem to think. We offered jobs, too, you'll notice."

"*Invented* jobs, you mean."

"Okay, we *could* have organized the library with volunteers. But there was a reason for coming up with jobs."

"I'd be glad to hear it."

"Well, for one thing, no one wanted to be responsible for supporting a bunch of women."

"Is that what you think marriage is?"

"Damn right."

Abbey swallowed tightly. "You've told me everything I need to know." Her voice broke on the last word, and Sawyer felt shaken.

He tensed, knowing he'd botched

this entire conversation. He wondered how he could explain the situation to her — without making things worse.

"It's lonely up here, Abbey. If you want to fault us for feeling like that, then go ahead. I was losing pilots left and right. Christian and I had to do *something* to keep them happy, and the only solution we could come up with was, uh, importing a few women." He knew that hadn't been the best way to put it, but he plunged on. "We wanted female companionship without the problems of marriage. We —"

"In other words, you wanted these 'imported' women to relieve the boredom." She closed her eyes as if he'd confirmed her worst fears.

"Did something happen today?" he asked, clenching his fists. "If anyone offended you, I'll personally see to it that he apologizes."

"*You've* offended me!" she cried.

"Why? Because I didn't offer to marry you? One woman's already tried to lure me into that trap."

"Trap?"

"I'm not going to marry you, Abbey, so if that's what you want, you'd better get this straight, right here and now. I brought you here so you'd be friends with a few of my men." Too late he realized how that must sound. "You know what I mean."

"I know *exactly* what you mean."

Sawyer could see that Abbey was

in no mood to be reasonable. She'd already made up her mind, and nothing he said would change it. "We'll settle this later," he said gruffly.

She didn't respond.

Sawyer had to force himself to leave the library. He started down the walk, paused and started back, then stopped again. What a mess. He hated unfinished business.

Scott rode down the street on Ronny Gold's bicycle and pulled to a stop beside him. "Hi, Sawyer!" he said enthusiastically.

Sawyer's gaze was still locked on the library door. "Hiya, Scott."

"How's it going?"

"Good," Sawyer lied.

"Ronny let me ride his bike. I'll

sure be glad when mine gets here. How much longer do you think it'll take the shippers to haul our stuff to Hard Luck?"

Sawyer's eyes reluctantly drifted from the library to the boy. It seemed heartless to tell him the truck wouldn't make it to town anytime this summer.

"You miss your bike, do you?"

"It'd be neat if I had it, 'cause then Ronny and I could ride together."

"I've got an old bike from when I was a kid. I think it's in the storage shed. Would you like me to see if I can find it for you?"

Scott's eyes lit up. "Gee, that'd be great!"

"I'll go look for it right away,"

Sawyer promised, eager for an opportunity to prove himself a family friend, instead of the fiend Abbey thought he was. He really didn't understand what had upset her so much. "I mean, what did she think when she answered the ad?" he muttered to himself.

It took some doing to locate the old bicycle, which was hidden in the back of the shed behind twenty years' worth of accumulated junk. Old though it was, the bike wasn't in bad shape.

Sawyer hosed it off in the front yard. When he finished the task, he happened to look up — and saw Abbey walking home.

He straightened, standing in the middle of his yard, the hose in his hand dripping water. He stared at her. With every bone, every muscle, every cell in his body, he ached to know what he'd done that was so wrong. More important, he needed to know how he could fix it.

Without even glancing in his direction, Abbey disappeared into the house. Not long afterward Scott approached him, frowning.

"The old bike doesn't look like much, does it?" Sawyer said, drying off the padded seat and chrome fender with an old T-shirt. "But I think once I get her cleaned up a bit and give the chain a shot of oil, it'll be fine."

"No, the bike looks great," Scott said, his sudden smile brimming with pleasure. But some of his enthusiasm faded when he looked over his shoulder. "I have to get home."

"If you wait a few minutes I'll have the bike ready for you."

"I better get home."

Sawyer nodded in the direction of his brother's house. "Your mother seems upset about something."

"I'll say," Scott said. "She's *real* upset."

Sawyer stared at the front door, and the ache inside him intensified. He wouldn't rest until he'd sorted out this business with Abbey. "Maybe I should try to talk to her."

"Not now, I wouldn't," the boy advised.

Sawyer realized — with some embarrassment — how inept he

was at dealing with women. Inept enough to accept advice from a nine-year-old boy. Still, if Scott thought it best to wait, he would.

"You'd think she'd be happy," Scott said with a long sigh. "Grandma and Grandpa kept telling her she should go out on dates, but Mom never wanted to. She went out sometimes, but not very often. Now she's all upset because some guy asked her to dinner."

"Who?" Sawyer demanded before he could censor the question. "Never mind, Scott, that's none of my business."

"Well, Grandma wants her to get married again. I heard them talking once, and Grandma was telling my mom that it's wrong to let one bad experience sour her on marriage. She said there were lots of good men in this world and Mom would find one of 'em if she tried. Do *you* think my mom should get married again?"

Marriage wasn't a subject Sawyer felt comfortable discussing. "I . . . I wouldn't know."

"Mom's never said anything to us, but I'm pretty sure she gets lonely sometimes. Did you know Mr. Livengood asked her to marry him today?"

"What?" A fierce, possessive anger consumed Sawyer. He threw down the hose and was halfway out of his yard before he realized he couldn't very well wring Pete's neck. No matter what his feelings toward

Abbey, Sawyer had no right to be angry. If Pete wanted to propose to her, that was his prerogative. He himself had no say in the matter.

"Scott!" Abbey had come out onto the porch to call her son. Sawyer might as well have been invisible for all the attention she paid him. "Dinnertime."

"In a minute, Mom."

"Now," she insisted.

"You'd better go," Sawyer said. "I'll bring the bike over after dinner."

"Okay." He dashed across the street, stopping when he reached the other side. "Sawyer," he called, "don't worry. Mom still likes you best."

Unfortunately the boy's opinion

was no comfort at all.

Abbey couldn't eat; the food stuck in her throat. It felt as if she was swallowing gravel. The baked salmon certainly felt that way in the pit of her stomach.

Scott and Susan had never seemed more talkative, but she found it difficult to respond to their comments and questions.

"Sawyer said I could use his bike until mine gets here," Scott said, glancing expectantly at Abbey.

She'd been such an idiot. It had taken her virtually the whole day to figure out what was happening. Every unmarried man in town — most of them, anyway — had made a point of visiting the library, and it wasn't to check out books. No, it had more to do with checking out the librarian.

The newspaper ad had claimed there were lonely men in Hard Luck, but that wasn't the reason she'd applied. Not at all!

"Isn't it neat of him to lend me his bike?" he asked.

Abbey had to think about the question before she could answer it. "Very nice."

"Did Mr. Livengood really ask you to marry him?" Susan piped up, her dark eyes wide with curiosity.

"Would you like some more rice?" Abbey asked, intent on changing the subject. The last thing she wanted to do was discuss the miserable details of her day.

"He said he was serious," Scott said. "I overheard him telling Mrs. Inman that he wanted to get his bid in before anyone else."

Abbey groaned. How many more proposals would she have to endure? Apparently Sawyer was the only man in Hard Luck who *wasn't* interested in marriage. His ridiculous comment about her trying to lure him into marriage still rankled. As if she'd even *consider* such a thing.

"Are you going to marry him?" Susan asked.

"Of course not. I barely know Mr. Livengood."

"I think you should marry Sawyer," Susan said thoughtfully. "Do

Scott and I get to choose a new husband for you? 'Cause if we do, I bet Scott'd want Sawyer, too."

"I am not marrying Sawyer O'Halloran," Abbey said, obviously with more vehemence than she'd intended, because both children gave her odd, confused looks.

"Why not?" Scott asked. "I like him."

"He told us a bedtime story and took us swimming and named a lake after you, Mom. Don't you think he'd be a good husband?"

Abbey's shoulders sagged. "Let's not talk about Sawyer right now, okay?"

Scott and Susan accepted her request without comment, for which Abbey was grateful. They both began to chatter about their new friends and their plans and Eagle Catcher and what they'd done that day.

She was grateful her children had adjusted so well to life in such a small community. A town that lacked the amenities and resources they were used to. She'd been certain they'd find plenty of reasons to miss Seattle. They hadn't, even though they'd left behind their friends, their grandparents, their whole lives.

So had she.

After dinner Abbey was sitting alone at the kitchen table, drinking coffee and reviewing the woeful events of her day, when there was a knock at the door. She answered it to find Sawyer standing on the stoop. Her heart thumped wildly.

His eyes held hers for so long it took her a minute to realize he had the bike her son had mentioned.

"Wait here and I'll get Scott," she told him.

A muscle worked in his jaw. "I brought the bike over for Scott, but it's you I want to talk to." Nothing showed in his eyes, but she felt the power of the emotions he held in check.

The same emotions churned inside her.

"Abbey, please. Tell me what happened today."

"You mean other than two invitations to dinner and a marriage proposal? Oh, I nearly forgot — I was invited to inspect one pilot's fishing flies."

Sawyer closed his eyes. "That'd be John."

"Right. John. There were gifts, too."

The muscle in his jaw jerked again. "Gifts?"

"A bit of inducement, I suspect."

"I apologize for the behavior of my men. If you want, I'll drag every one of 'em down here to apologize."

"That's not what I want," she said coldly.

He heard the phone ring, and with unconcealed relief, Abbey went to answer it.

Sawyer took the mail run into Fairbanks himself. He found he could think more clearly when he was in the air. The roar of the plane's engines drowned out everything but the thoughts whirling inside his head.

He'd heard there were only two laws a pilot needed to concern himself with. The laws of gravity and of averages. Whoever had said that hadn't taken into account the laws of nature — of physical attraction between a man and a woman.

Abbey confused him. Never had he been this attracted to a woman. The few kisses they'd shared had been a shock to his senses. He imagined the excitement, the satisfaction, of making love to her. . . .

Yes, he wanted Abbey. But even a

saint couldn't find fault with the way he'd behaved toward her.

Frustration gnawed at him, eating away at his confidence. Granted, he hadn't been completely in favor of Christian's plan, but he didn't think it was unethical or unfair. It wasn't a question of false pretenses. Well, except for the cabins, which they had — slightly — misrepresented. He didn't want to force anyone, man *or* woman, into a relationship. Not everyone wanted to become romantically involved; it was a personal decision. This way there was no pressure, but for the life of him, he couldn't make Abbey understand that. Offering women jobs instead of marriage meant everyone had a choice when it came to romance. Surely that was as much to the women's benefit as the men's!

The mere thought of her accusations infuriated him. He'd noticed it hadn't taken her long to bring up the subject of marriage.

Did he want to marry her? Did he love her?

Somehow Sawyer found it easier not just to think at thirteen thousand feet but to confront his emotions. What did he know about love? Not much, he decided. From his earliest memories, his parents had been at odds. He felt sure that his parents had genuinely cared for each other, but in every other way theirs had been a bad match. Bringing his mother from the sophistication of London, England, to a primitive little community like Hard Luck couldn't have helped, either. Ellen had gone back to England, taking Christian with her, when Sawyer was thirteen. He'd never forgotten the desolate look on his father's face when the plane took off with his mother and youngest brother aboard.

It was the one and only time Sawyer could ever remember his father getting drunk. And he realized now, as an adult, that it was regret he'd seen in David's eyes.

Sawyer was well aware, as was Charles, when their father began seeing Catherine Fletcher. He often wondered if David would have filed for divorce had Ellen not returned.

At first everything was better. His parents had decided to make a new start, and for a while, life in the O'Halloran household was smoother and more pleasant than it had ever been. Sawyer had missed his youngest brother and his mother. At fourteen he hadn't understood the nature of his parents' relationship; all he knew was that he and his brothers were happy. Ellen had come back. They were a family again.

Unfortunately it didn't last. Everything suddenly changed, and his mother moved out of their bedroom. To the best of Sawyer's knowledge, Ellen and David never slept in the same room again. Later, after the lodge was built, they didn't even sleep in the same house.

No one needed to tell Sawyer why this had happened. His mother had learned about David's affair with Catherine. No one needed to tell him how she'd found out, either. Catherine had taken pleasure in breaking his mother's heart, destroying the tentative beginnings of happiness.

Sawyer had never understood why his parents didn't divorce. In the end, it was almost as if they'd *looked* for ways to make each other miserable.

No, his parents hadn't taught him about love. Nor had he learned much about it in the years since.

Until Abbey . . .

His mind filled with thoughts of her and Scott and Susan. If she was so distraught about her agreement to work in Hard Luck, he'd release her from any obligation, real or imagined. She was free to go. He'd personally escort her and the children to Fairbanks and see them off.

His heart beat high in his throat at the possibility of losing Abbey.

But if Sawyer admitted he loved her, he'd have to make a decision, and he wasn't ready for that either. They'd met less than two weeks ago. One thing was certain, though — he could no longer picture Hard Luck without her.

When Sawyer returned later that afternoon, he found Scott riding the old bicycle at the airfield. He spotted Eagle Catcher first and smiled to himself as he taxied the Cessna over to the hangar.

"You sure do fly good," Scott told him with admiration when he climbed down from the cockpit.

"Thank you, Scott."

"Are you going to take me up with you like you said?"

"Yeah, someday."

The boy's face fell. "That's what you said last time."

Sawyer remembered how much he'd disliked being put off when he was a kid. "You're right, Scott. I did say you could fly with me. Let's check the schedule."

"You mean it?"

"Yes, but we'll have to ask your

mother's permission first."

Scott kicked the dirt with the toe of his sneaker. "I don't think you're her favorite person right now."

"She's still mad, is she?"

"Yup. She told Mr. Livengood she wasn't interested in marrying him. He looked like he was real disappointed, but you know what? I think he would've been surprised if she said yes."

"Maybe I should talk to her." Or try, although heaven knew he'd done that often enough.

"I wouldn't," the boy said.

"Well, have you got any other ideas, then?" Sawyer resigned himself to asking a nine-year-old boy for advice.

"The other guys brought her

dumb gifts. Mom doesn't care about bug spray. She doesn't like mosquitoes, but we've gotten real good at keeping them away."

"Okay, I won't give her any bug spray. Can you think of anything she'd like?"

"Sure," Scott said. "She likes long baths with those smelly things that melt."

"Smelly things that melt? What are those?"

"Bath-oil beads," Scott said. "If you can get her those, she might listen to you."

It was worth a try. He'd hit a drugstore next trip to Fairbanks. He walked into the office and held the door open for Scott to follow. Everyone had left for the day, which suited Sawyer fine.

He sat down at his desk; Scott sat in the opposite chair. Leaning back, Sawyer propped his feet on the corner and linked his hands behind his head. Scott imitated his actions, knobby elbows sticking out like miniature moose antlers from the sides of his head.

There was a knock at the door, and Susan poked her head inside. Her smile widened. "Hi, Sawyer," she said. "I saw your bike outside," she told her brother. "Mom wants you."

"What for?" he asked.

"She needs you to help her carry some stuff home from the library."

"Okay," Scott said. He released a long-suffering sigh.

"Want me to come with you?" Sawyer offered. He didn't think Abbey would appreciate it, but then he hadn't seen her all day. Maybe, just maybe, she'd missed him as much as he'd missed her, and they could put this unpleasantness behind them.

"It's okay," Scott assured him. "I can do it." He started toward the door.

"I appreciate the advice, Scott. Next run I make into Fairbanks, I'll buy plenty of those smelly bath things for your mom."

"Uh, Sawyer." Scott's face broke into a grin. "There's something else you could do."

"What's that?"

Scott and Susan exchanged looks.

"You could always marry my mom," the boy said. "Of all the guys who've proposed so far, we like you the best."

CHAPTER 8

So Pete Livengood wasn't the only one who'd popped the question, Sawyer mused darkly. Scott and Susan had said as much, and they were in a position to know. It infuriated him that the men in this community would make such asses of themselves over the first woman to arrive. These were the very men who'd insisted all they wanted was a little female companionship. Yet the minute Abbey set foot in town, they were stumbling all over themselves to see which of them could marry her first.

What bothered him even more were his own confused feelings for Abbey. He didn't want any of the other men in town approaching her — offering her gifts, dinner dates, marriage proposals. No, if anyone was going to do those things, he wanted it to be him. He just wasn't sure about the marriage part; he *was* sure about wanting to see Abbey. On an exclusive basis.

There, he'd owned up to it. But from the looks she'd given him lately, she'd rather go out with a rattlesnake than with him.

He sulked for a few minutes before leaving the office. He wondered if Mitch Harris had taken a liking to Abbey, too. Mitch hardly knew Abbey, but then, that hadn't stopped Pete from proposing. Mitch, a widower, was a good guy. Chrissie Harris and Susan had been hanging around together; he hoped that wouldn't give Mitch an unfair advantage.

There were a number of other unmarried men in town. Ben Hamilton, for one. The owner of the Hard Luck Café was around the same age as Pete Livengood, and Sawyer considered him a good friend. But that didn't mean Ben didn't have eyes in his head. Abbey was a beautiful woman, and Sawyer could understand why any man would be attracted to her.

There was no telling how many

had lined up to offer Abbey their hearts and their homes. Not that he had any right to complain. It was more than he'd done. And a whole lot more than he intended to do.

Marriage was a lifetime commitment. Make that a life sentence. In his experience, marriage meant the death of love. It had killed whatever love his parents had started out with. Well, he wouldn't let that happen to him. No, sirree. He was frustrated and annoyed that the men of Hard Luck were so careless about their freedom.

As he continued his unsatisfying reflections, Sawyer strolled over to Ben's. It was too early for the dinner crowd, such as it was, and too late for lunch. The café was empty.

Sawyer slid onto a stool and up-righted a mug.

Almost immediately, Ben appeared from the kitchen and reached for the coffeepot. "What's bugging you?"

Sawyer smiled to himself, amused and rather impressed that the cook could read him so easily. "How'd you know something's bothering me?"

"You came in for coffee, right?"

"Right."

"You got a pot at your office, same as I do here. I know I'm a good-lookin' cuss, but I don't think you'd be willing to pay a buck-fifty for a cup of coffee unless you needed to talk. What's up?"

"It's that obvious?"

"Yeah." Ben picked up the empty sugar canister and refilled it.

Sawyer didn't know where to begin. He didn't want to let on that what he'd really come here to learn was whether Ben had proposed to Abbey, along with everyone else in town.

"Let me help you out," Ben said when he'd finished with the sugar canister. "A man doesn't wear that damned-if-you-do damned-if-you-don't look smeared across his face unless a woman's involved. Is it Abbey?"

"Yeah." Sawyer couldn't see any reason to deny it. "Pete Livengood proposed to her." He raised the coffee mug and studied Ben's reaction through the rising steam. The cook gave nothing away.

"So I heard."

"Apparently a few other men in town had the same idea."

Ben chuckled and brushed the sugar from his palms. "Someone else being interested in Abbey upsets you?"

That was putting it mildly. "Well, you could say I'm concerned," Sawyer admitted grudgingly.

Ben leaned against the counter, obviously waiting for him to proceed.

"I know what you're going to say," Sawyer said before Ben could prod him. "You want to know what's holding me back. If I'm so worried Abbey'll marry someone

352

else, why don't I propose myself? For a number of very good reasons, if you must know," he said, raising his voice. "First and foremost, I refuse to be forced into this. A man doesn't offer marriage lightly, or at least he shouldn't." He was thinking of Pete and the others. "Another thing. I won't have any woman dictating to me what I should and shouldn't do with my life."

Ben's face creased with a smug look. "Why are you yelling at me?"

Sawyer shut his eyes for a moment and shook his head helplessly. "Darned if I know." Once again, he found himself thinking about his own parents and how miserable they'd been together. Abbey had already been married once. Badly burned, too, as far as he could tell.

The cocky smile vanished from Ben's face. "Maybe what you need to figure out is if you love her."

That debate had been going on inside him all day. "I don't *know* what I feel," he blurted out.

"What about her kids?"

Some of the tension left him. "I'm crazy about those two."

Ben studied him as if seeing Sawyer in a whole new light. "You didn't think you'd ever really fall for a woman, did you? The fact is, before Abbey and her children got here, you thought you were happy."

"I am happy," Sawyer insisted.

"Sure you are," Ben muttered. Chuckling to himself, he returned to the kitchen.

"I'm damn happy," Sawyer shouted after him.

"Right," Ben called back. The old coot seemed highly amused. "You're so happy you're crying in your coffee, afraid Abbey Sutherland's going to marry someone else. Careful, Sawyer, she just might, and then what'll you do?"

Sawyer slapped a handful of coins down on the counter and stomped out.

Abbey inserted a card into the catalog and reached for the next one. This low-tech approach to librarianship was a far cry from the computerized system she was used to, but for the moment, it was manageable. She glanced up as the door opened and Pearl Inman stepped in. "Are you coming down to the airfield?" she asked. "John Henderson's due back any time with Allison Reynolds."

"Give me a minute."

"I don't know about you, but I'm looking forward to meeting this young woman," Pearl said. "Ben baked a cake to welcome her. I just hope the men don't make fools of themselves the way they did when you got here."

Abbey's heart fluttered with a mixture of dread and excitement as she pulled on her sweater and headed out the door. She was eager to meet Allison, eager to have another woman move to Hard Luck.

If she remembered correctly, Allison was the woman Christian had mentioned the night he'd phoned — his dinner date.

It was inevitable that she'd run into Sawyer at the airfield; avoiding him in a town the size of Hard Luck was impossible. Nor did she wish to. She'd been angry and upset the last time they spoke. She wasn't accustomed to a lot of attention from men — it flustered and alarmed her. Then, without intending to, Sawyer had made everything worse. What upset her most was the way he'd insinuated she was hoping to trap him into marriage.

Despite what Sawyer might have thought, she *wasn't* planning to

357

remarry. When she'd applied for the job, she'd done so because that was what she needed — a job. Going to Alaska had sounded adventurous, and small-town life had appealed to her. She *hadn't* come to "be friendly" to a bunch of love-starved men.

Unfortunately, once her children learned that Pete Livengood had proposed to her, they'd jumped on the bandwagon. Not that they wanted her to marry Pete. Oh, no, they were campaigning for Sawyer. Both Scott and Susan made sure they casually dropped his name at every opportunity. It was Sawyer this and Sawyer that, until she was sick of hearing about him. Abbey didn't have the heart to tell them he was the last man she'd marry — even if he asked her. Not with that attitude of his. He'd always believe she'd tricked him into marriage.

The day was overcast and cool, a contrast to the warm sunshine the area had enjoyed all week. Shivering a little, she walked to the airfield with Pearl.

Half the town was there waiting for the plane's arrival. Scott pulled up next to her on Sawyer's old bicycle, shading his eyes as he gazed up into the sky.

"What's the big deal?" he asked.

"Sawyer's new secretary's coming."

"Does she have any kids?"

The question amused Abbey. She wondered what Sawyer would do if another woman showed up on his doorstep with a family in tow.

"Probably not," she said.

"Are the men gonna want to marry her, too?"

"Maybe."

"What about Sawyer?"

"I wouldn't know," she answered, more emphatically this time.

"We want *you* to marry Sawyer," her son persisted. "Susan and me like him a whole lot, and he likes us."

"Scott, please!"

"But if he might marry this new lady, don't you think you should do something about it?"

"No," she said in her sternest voice, praying no one was listening in on their conversation.

"I hear the plane," Pearl shouted.

Abbey squinted into the hazy skies. She heard the buzz of an approaching aircraft, but couldn't see anything just yet. She recalled the excitement she'd felt when she'd flown into Hard Luck and looked down to find such a large welcoming committee.

The plane appeared over the horizon and slowly descended toward the dirt runway. Once it had taxied to a stop, Duke Porter hurried over and lowered the steps.

A minute later, a woman dressed in a hot-pink silk jumpsuit moved slowly down the steps. Like royalty, Abbey thought.

Allison Reynolds was beautiful, she saw with a small pang of jealousy. Knock-your-eyes-out gorgeous. Long legs that seemed to reach all the way to her earlobes, a more-than-ample bosom and a body that would stop New York City traffic. Allison gave a beauty-queen wave and the smile she bestowed on the crowd of welcomers was bright enough to create a glare.

Abbey suspected every man present was wiping drool off his chin. Until that moment, she'd avoided looking for Sawyer, but now she scanned the crowd, seeking him out. She found him, his intense blue eyes glued to the latest arrival with undeniable interest. Just like the others.

Her heart chilled as she admitted to herself that he really wasn't any different. Disillusioned — and determined to ignore it — she squared her shoulders and looked away.

Lonely men, indeed. Well, they were getting what they wanted with Allison Reynolds. Thank heaven.

Just as they had the day Abbey and the kids came, everyone assembled at the Hard Luck Café for introductions. Allison Reynolds was ushered inside and seated while the town put forth its best effort to impress her.

Abbey stood back and waited for a chance to welcome her. From her position by the wall, she had a clear view of the newcomer. Abbey sincerely hoped she and Allison would be friends. At the moment she could do with a friend.

"I'd like to talk to you."

Abbey started, then turned to discover Sawyer standing next to her. "Do you always sneak up behind people?" she asked in an angry whisper.

"Only when I'm desperate." He leaned one shoulder against the wall and crossed his arms. "It's Mitch Harris, isn't it?"

"What is?"

"The other man who proposed."

"That's none of your business."

"I'm making it my business. Was it Mitch?" he growled in a low whisper. Then not giving her time to answer, he asked again. "What about Ben Hamilton? I wouldn't put it past the old goat. He prob-

ably did it just to rile me." He
sighed, shaking his head. "It
worked, too."

"As I said earlier, none of this
concerns you." If there'd been
anywhere to move, Abbey would
have moved, but the café was
packed. Why on earth would Sawyer choose this precise minute to
talk to her?

"You aren't marrying any of
them."

"I beg your pardon?"

"I'm serious, Abbey. Call me a
male chauvinist or whatever else
you want, but if you're so intent on
finding a husband, I'll marry you
myself." His voice was harsh.

"You'll marry me yourself?" she
asked, incredulous. "How generous

of you. How benevolent!"

"I mean it," he said.

"Tell me, Sawyer, why would you do anything so . . . so drastic?" Mingled with her anger was a pain that cut deep, despite her disenchantment. This was exactly the type of behavior she'd come to expect from Sawyer — yet she was disappointed.

Her question appeared to hit its mark. His face tensed and the muscle in his jaw leapt. Unable to listen to any more, Abbey walked out of the café. She'd introduce herself to Allison later.

She'd gone only a few feet when she heard the screen door slam behind her. Quickening her steps, she hurried away.

"Abbey, wait!"

Half a minute later, he'd caught up with her. "For heaven's sake, will you stop long enough to listen to me?"

Her throat was so clogged with tears, it was impossible to answer him. He steered her onto the airfield and into a nearby hangar, then turned to face her. His outstretched arms touched her shoulder.

Abbey kept her face averted, praying he'd say whatever he intended to say so she could leave.

"Why do I want to marry you?" He sounded as confused as she did.

"You don't want me," she accused. "All you care about is making sure I don't accept anyone else's proposal. Your ridiculous male pride couldn't take that! Well, if you thought you were appeasing me with this insulting offer of marriage, you're dead wrong."

"I do want you," he argued, pulling her into his arms.

Her heart stopped, then jerked back to life as he directed her mouth to his. The kiss was long and thorough. Groaning softly, he kissed her again, hungrily this time. Her lips parted, and she slid her arms tightly around his hard waist.

They engaged in a series of warm, moist kisses that became more and more intense. He drew her closer until the full lengths of their bodies were pressed together. She felt the rise and fall of his chest and knew her own breathing was as labored.

Suddenly, looking stunned, he dragged his mouth from hers. He dropped his hands, releasing her, and stepped back.

Abbey studied him for a moment. "Don't look so worried, Sawyer," she said with wounded dignity. "I'm not going to accept your proposal." She spun on her heel and walked away, grateful he chose not to follow her.

As it happened, Abbey got a chance to talk to Allison Reynolds later that same afternoon. They met in the road outside the library. After a few minutes' conversation, it was apparent — at least to Abbey — that the other woman had no intention of staying in Hard Luck and probably never had.

"You're Abbey," Allison said, smiling. "Christian told me he'd hired you." She crossed her arms and swatted at a mosquito. "Can we talk?" Allison asked, doing a poor imitation of Joan Rivers. "I'm dying to find out how things have gone for you since you arrived." Allison glanced both ways, then lowered her voice conspiratorially. "Are you going to stay?"

"I plan to. So far, I love Alaska."

"But it's summer," Allison said as if this was something Abbey hadn't yet figured out. "I don't think anyone was serious about us staying all winter, do you? I mean, this is the *Arctic.* I don't go anywhere in the winter where there isn't a hot tub."

"I've never lived through an Arctic winter before, so I can't say, but I do know I'm going to try."

"You are?" The new secretary for Midnight Sons spoke as though Abbey was making a serious mistake. "Anyway, I can't talk long. I'm supposed to meet Ralph and Pearl, and they're going to drive me out to the cabin. I've never had a home of my own. Christian said it's a quaint little place. I can hardly wait to see it. But I do hope someone finds a way to get the rest of my luggage up here soon. They seemed to think I could pack everything in three suitcases."

Before Abbey could describe her own experience, Allison was gone.

Actually Abbey was just as glad not to be around when Allison viewed her "quaint" new home.

The rest of the afternoon passed slowly, the main attraction being the vivacious and beautiful Allison Reynolds and not the newly opened Hard Luck Lending Library.

Pearl Inman was watering her cabbage plants when Abbey walked past on her way home.

"What a sorry disappointment Allison Reynolds is," Pearl Inman muttered. "That Christian's got mush for brains. I can't imagine what he was thinking when he hired her."

Abbey grinned. "Himself most likely."

"That girl got a free trip to Alaska

— which was all she wanted," Pearl said with a disgruntled look. "Makes me downright angry to think of the way everyone's been so excited about meeting her."

"She might change her mind and stay."

"It'd be a mistake if she did. Allison Reynolds is the type who causes more problems than she solves. My guess is she'll be out of here before the week's up."

Personally Abbey agreed with Pearl.

"I saw you and Sawyer talking. I'm glad to hear you decided to put that boy out of his misery."

Abbey wasn't aware that her troubles with Sawyer were common knowledge. "If Sawyer O'Halloran's miserable, he has no one to blame but himself."

"Isn't that the way it is with most folks?"

Abbey had no argument there.

"As for what happened to you this week, with the men and all, well —" Pearl sighed "— I have to say I blame Sawyer for that."

"So do I," Abbey said. And if he assumed he could make everything better by tossing her a marriage proposal, he was mistaken.

"The men wouldn't have come at you like a herd of buffalo if Sawyer hadn't tried to keep you for himself," Pearl was saying. "Way I hear it, some of them were up in arms because of all the rules and restrictions he put on them."

"Rules?"

"He didn't want anyone pestering you. However, he didn't include himself in that. But this is the only time I've ever seen Sawyer take advantage of a situation. You know," the older woman said thoughtfully, "I don't think he realized he was doing it. His intentions were to help you and the children get settled. I know for a fact that he never expected to fall in love with you."

Abbey looked away to hide her sudden tears. Sawyer *didn't* love her. His proposal told her that much. He was afraid she'd accept someone else, so he'd put his offer on the table. Only a day earlier, he'd vehemently insisted he wasn't marrying anyone.

"I'll see you later, Pearl," Abbey murmured.

Her friend cast her a look of concern. "You okay, sweetie?"

Abbey nodded, but she wasn't. What truly frightened her was that she'd fallen in love with Sawyer. Fallen fast and fallen hard. Once before, she'd proved what a poor judge of character she was when it came to men. She'd left the marriage broken, her confidence destroyed. She blinked back the tears that stung her eyes, feeling a strange new desolation.

Abbey was nearly home when she noticed a truck driving toward her. She knew almost everyone in town by now and stared at the unfamiliar

— yet somewhat familiar — face as the truck slowed to a stop.

"Hello," the driver said.

"Hello," she responded, sniffling a bit.

"I'm Charles O'Halloran."

"Abbey Sutherland," she whispered.

Charles frowned. "Do you mind telling me what's going on around here?"

Sawyer sat in his office, rolling a pen between his palms. Every time he talked to Abbey he made matters worse. It started when he saw her standing on the airfield waiting for Allison Reynolds. His heart had actually hurt at the sight of her. Even now he didn't know what he'd done that was so terrible, and Abbey wouldn't tell him.

A man had his pride, but he'd been willing to swallow it one more time, so he'd followed her into Ben's place. Then, before he could stop himself, he was drilling her about other men, acting like a lunatic. He'd never been jealous in his life, and he didn't know how to handle it. John, Pete, Duke, Ralph, Mitch and the other guys were his friends. Or had been.

The office door opened and without a word of warning, in stepped his oldest brother. "Charles!" Sawyer bolted to his feet. "Hey, it's good to see you! When'd you get in?"

"About an hour ago." Charlie

slipped the backpack from his shoulders and set it aside.

Charles looked tanned and healthy. He was a leaner, taller version of Sawyer, people often said.

Walking over to the coffeepot, Charles poured himself a mug.

Sawyer knew his brother well enough to recognize that he was upset. "You got a problem?"

His brother sighed and sipped his coffee. "Can you explain how you and Christian managed to let your brains go all soggy in the space of a few weeks?"

Sawyer laughed. "So you heard about the women."

"That's exactly what I'm talking about."

"We flew them here. And there's

more coming."

"To live?"

Sawyer nodded, the humor leaving him. Just as he'd expected, Charles didn't think much of their scheme. "We came up with the idea of offering them those old cabins Dad built, plus twenty acres of land. In exchange, they have to live and work in Hard Luck for a year." As he spoke, Sawyer realized how ludicrous the idea must sound to their levelheaded older brother. It had to him at first, too, but his arguments had grown less convincing after Abbey's arrival.

"The women are supposed to *live* in those old cabins?" Charles asked incredulously.

"We cleaned them out, Charlie.

They're actually quite . . . clean."

With unexpected violence, Charles slammed down his mug. "Have you two lost your minds?"

"No. We did what we thought was necessary to help the community grow." Sawyer was aware that he came across as stiff and pompous.

"It wasn't Hard Luck you were thinking about when you advertised for women," Charles countered. "You were thinking of yourselves."

"We were losing pilots left and right," Sawyer snapped. "Phil's gone, and we were about to lose Ralph and John as well. The men were willing to stay if we could bring in a few women."

"How many do you have coming?"

"I don't know," Sawyer confessed, trying to suppress his own anger. "Christian took care of that end of it."

"Was it Christian who sent up the beauty queen, or are you the one responsible for that?"

"Beauty queen? Oh, you mean Allison. No, she was Christian's idea. Okay, she probably won't work out. We're bound to have a few failures, but that's the law of averages. Some women are going to adjust and become part of our community. Others won't."

"Allison Reynolds wants out of the deal. Claims she was sold a false bill of goods. I talked to her myself — ran into her at Ben's."

"Fine. I told you, I didn't expect

her to last. I'll arrange for her flight back to Seattle. All I have to do is tell Christian, and he can send up another secretary. From what I understand, there are plenty of applicants."

"Which brings up something else neither of you seemed to trouble yourself with. The media."

Sawyer had gotten a number of inquiries, but he'd steadfastly refused to give interviews. Way up here, he felt relatively safe from the press.

"You aren't so naive as to think the press doesn't know, are you?" Charles asked.

"Of course they know," Sawyer answered. "But they didn't hear about it from me. Before long, it'll be old news and everyone'll leave us alone."

"For your information," Charles said tersely, "I read about your scheme in the Anchorage newspaper while I was in Valdez."

"Okay, so the news is out," Sawyer muttered, unconcerned. He had more important things to worry about than some unwanted publicity.

"How do you think the media are going to react when they learn you've already got a failure on your hands? These women don't know anything about Alaska. They left everything they had and flew up here, thinking God knows what and expecting something far different than they were promised."

"Okay, Allison's a failure, and frankly that's Christian's fault. But Abbey Sutherland's one of the best things that's ever happened to Hard Luck. She's already got the library organized and in operation."

"Abbey Sutherland's the one living in Christian's house, right?"

"Yes." He didn't think now was the time to admit the mistake they'd made with the application form. Nor did he want Charles to know he'd contacted Catherine Fletcher's daughter about the use of Catherine's home for Abbey and her children.

"It seems you've misjudged the situation with her."

Sawyer's head snapped up. "Just what do you mean by that?"

"She isn't staying."

Sawyer's eyes narrowed. "Who told you that?"

"Abbey herself."

Sawyer felt as if he'd had the wind knocked out of him. It took a long moment before he could think clearly. "You met Abbey?"

Charles nodded.

"She's staying," Sawyer said, not waiting to hear his brother's argument.

"Sawyer, damn it, will you listen to reason?" Charles shouted.

"I couldn't care less what Allison Reynolds decides," he told his brother. "But Abbey and her kids are staying."

Charles groaned. "She has children?"

Sawyer rushed toward the door.

"Where are you going?" his brother demanded.

"To see Abbey."

He made the trek between the office and Christian's place in record time. He arrived, breathless with anger and exertion, at her front door, his shoulders heaving. Instead of knocking, he hammered his fist against the door.

Abbey answered it and stared at him through the screen.

"You aren't leaving." His voice was a harsh whisper.

"Sawyer," Charles shouted from behind him. "What do you think you're doing?" He leapt up the porch steps. "We've already talked about you going back to Seattle, remember?" he said to Abbey, lowering his voice.

Abbey stood on the other side of the screen door, her hand over her mouth.

It was all Sawyer could do not to rip the door off its hinges and haul her into his arms. "Abbey, listen, I —"

"Sawyer, leave the poor woman alone," Charles broke in.

Sawyer whirled around. "Stay out of this, Charles. This has nothing to do with you and everything to do with me." The two men glared at each other.

"Abbey," Charles said, looking past his brother. "Like I said, you don't have to live in Hard Luck if you don't want to. I'll personally pay for your tickets back to Seattle."

"I said I'd marry you," Sawyer reminded her, his voice raised. "Isn't that what you want?" His brother's words felt like a knife between his shoulder blades.

"No. It isn't what I want." With that, she started to close the door.

"Abbey," he cried, frantic to talk some sense into her.

The door closed. He fought back the temptation to open it and follow her inside.

The realization hit him that he was going to lose her, and there wasn't anything he could do about it. The last time he'd experienced such a feeling of hopelessness was the afternoon his father died.

Chapter 9

"What's for dinner?" Scott asked on his way through the kitchen. He didn't give Abbey time to answer. "Can we have macaroni and cheese? Not from a box, but the kind you bake in the oven?"

"Sure." Abbey kept her back to her son, trying to disguise how upset she was. Her hands were shaking and her eyes were brimming with tears.

All the contradictory emotions that had buffeted her for the past few days had reduced her to a help-less inertia. For the first time since her divorce, Abbey had allowed herself to fall in love — with a man who didn't know how to love, who didn't *want* to love.

Allison Reynolds was going to leave. She was the smart one, Ab-bey thought bitterly. The one who owned up to a mistake and took measures to correct it. That was what Abbey should've done — only earlier, much earlier, before her heart became so completely in-volved.

She'd made one devastating mis-take by marrying Dick. She'd known it almost immediately, but instead of admitting her error, she'd tried to make the best of a bad situation. She'd had to struggle for years afterward to get her life back in shape.

Then, a few weeks ago, she'd begun to dream again, to hope, to believe it was possible to find happiness with a man. Her illusions had been painfully shattered, one by one. It'd all started when she realized her position as Hard Luck's librarian had been a ruse — she'd been brought to Alaska to provide "female companionship" to a bunch of love-starved bush pilots.

Sawyer didn't want her to leave; she wasn't sure why and knew he wasn't, either. He was resisting whatever feelings he had for her, resenting them. He'd offered to marry her, but from the way he'd proposed, he seemed to consider marriage to Abbey some kind of punishment.

"Can Eagle Catcher come inside while we eat?" Scott asked, breaking into her thoughts.

Despite her misery, Abbey smiled. "You know the answer to that."

"But, Mom," Scott said in a sing-song voice, "I was hoping you'd change your mind. Eagle Catcher may be a dog on the outside, but on the inside he's a regular guy."

Her son lingered in the kitchen. He poked through cupboards, then opened the refrigerator and took out a pitcher of juice to pour himself a glass. "I saw you talking to some strange man earlier. In a truck." Scott waited as if he expected her to fill him in on the details. When she didn't, he added, "I thought it was Sawyer at first, but he doesn't have a beard."

She sighed. "That was Charles O'Halloran, Sawyer's brother."

"Oh." Scott pulled out a chair and sat down at the table. He didn't say anything for a long moment. Finally he asked, "Are you all right, Mom?"

"Sure," she said with forced enthusiasm. "Where's Susan?"

"She's playing with Chrissie Harris, like always. Do you want me to get her?"

"In a bit."

Scott finished off his juice, then headed for the back door. "Don't be late for dinner," she called after him.

"I won't, especially if we're having macaroni and cheese."

Her mind preoccupied with her own problems, Abbey thought it was quite an accomplishment that she didn't burn dinner. In spite of her earlier resolve to stay, in spite of the fact that she'd invested everything she had in moving here, Abbey came to a decision. By the time her children trooped in, the table was set and she was ready to address the unpleasant task of telling them they'd be leaving Hard Luck. Abbey knew Scott and Susan weren't going to like it.

They sat down at the dinner table together, and Abbey waited until they were halfway through the meal before broaching the subject. "I hear Allison Reynolds has decided she doesn't want to stay," she said casually. "She's flying out first thing in the morning."

"The new lady looked like a ditz to me," Scott commented between mouthfuls of macaroni and cheese.

"She's real pretty," Susan said.

"She's dumb."

"Scott!" Abbey interjected.

"Well, she is. Anyone who didn't like this place after we threw a party for her is more than dumb, she's *rude.*"

"Allison looked nice, though," Susan said. She stopped eating and studied Abbey.

Scott seemed far more concerned

with shoveling in as much macaroni and cheese as possible, as quickly as possible. If Abbey had been a betting woman, she'd have said Eagle Catcher was on the front porch waiting for him.

"You know," Abbey said carefully. "I'm not so sure it's the right place for us, either."

"You gotta be kidding!" Scott cried. "I like it here. I was kinda worried if I'd find new friends when we got here. But it's neat being the new kid on the block. Everyone wants to be my friend, and now that Sawyer let me have his old bike, it's like being back home."

"There's no ice-cream man," Susan said, gesturing with her fork. She continued to study Abbey.

"There's no place for us to live, either. When Mr. O'Halloran offered me the job, I didn't tell him I had a family."

"Why can't we stay right here?" Susan wanted to know. "This is a nice house."

"Because it belongs to Sawyer's brother Christian," Scott answered for her. "Sawyer told me he was going to phone some old lady who used to live in town. He thinks we should be able to rent her house. We don't have a problem, Mom. Sawyer's taking care of everything."

"It's not just the living arrangements," Abbey went on. "The trucking company can only take our furniture as far as Fairbanks. There's no way to get it to Hard

Luck until winter."

"I can wait," Scott volunteered.

"Me, too," Susan agreed.

"What about our supplies for winter?" she asked.

Both children stared at her as if she were speaking another language. "What does everyone else do?" Scott asked.

"They buy enough supplies to last them a year. Best as I can figure, that'd be nearly five thousand dollars for the three of us. I can't afford that."

"Can't you get a loan?" Scott suggested.

"No. I didn't know any of this, and now, well, it just makes sense for us to go back home."

"But Sawyer —"

"Please," she said, cutting Scott off. The last person she wanted to hear about was Sawyer. But she could see it was going to take more than excuses to convince her family they had to leave Hard Luck.

"I'm beginning to think we made a mistake in coming here," she whispered, barely able to look across the table at her children.

"A mistake? No way!"

"We *like* it here!" Susan protested.

"It's been a wonderful experience," Abbey said, "but it's time to stand back and assess the situation. We have some important decisions to make."

"You already made the decision," Scott insisted. "Don't you remember what you told us? You said that no matter what, we'd give it a year, and then we'd decide what we wanted to do. It isn't even a full month yet and you're already talking about quitting."

"There are things you don't understand," Abbey said. No one had told her that when she agreed to move to Alaska, she'd be putting her heart at risk. She would never have taken the gamble had she known the stakes were so high.

Over the past few weeks, she'd learned she could live without indoor plumbing. She could manage without electricity. She could do without the luxury of a shopping mall close at hand. But she could not tolerate another man crushing her heart.

And Sawyer would.

He didn't know about love, didn't trust it. His parents' difficult marriage had left him wary and cautious; she wasn't much better.

She'd taken all the pain she could bear from one man. She wasn't giving Sawyer the opportunity to take over where Dick had left off. As cowardly as it was, she'd made up her mind to leave.

She didn't expect her children to understand or appreciate that, which made everything so much more difficult.

"You aren't serious about moving, are you, Mom?"

Abbey swallowed past the tightness in her throat and nodded.

"I thought you liked it here,"

Susan wailed.

Everyone stopped eating. Scott and Susan stared at her, their eyes huge and forlorn.

"It just isn't working out the way I hoped," she told them brokenly.

"Is it because of Sawyer?" Scott asked.

Preferring not to lie, Abbey didn't answer him. "Since you both enjoy Alaska so much . . . I was thinking we could find a place in Fairbanks. Since that's where the truck's delivering our furniture, I thought we could rent a house and . . . and settle in before school starts again."

"I don't want to live in Fairbanks," Susan said emphatically. "I want to live here."

"I'm not leaving Eagle Catcher,"

Scott told her in a deceptively calm voice. From past experience, Abbey knew it wouldn't be easy to change her son's mind.

"There'll be lots of dogs in Fairbanks."

Susan began to sob. "Why do we have to leave?" she asked.

"Because . . . because we have to. Hard Luck is a wonderful town with friendly people, but . . . but it hasn't worked out for us."

"Why not?" Scott pressed. "I thought you liked it, too. Sawyer even named a lake after you, remember?"

There wasn't much she *didn't* remember about her times with Sawyer. The emotion that had hovered so close to the surface all day broke through, and hot, blistering tears filled her eyes.

"I'm so sorry . . ." Angry with herself for succumbing to her emotions, Abbey swiped at her face and drew in a deep breath, hoping it would relieve some of her tension.

"Why are you crying, Mommy?" Susan asked, sniffling herself.

Abbey patted her daughter's shoulder and stood up to reach for a couple of tissues.

"Is this because of Sawyer?" Scott demanded for the second time. "Is *he* the one who made you cry?"

"No. No!"

"You were mad at him before."

Abbey didn't need to be reminded of Sawyer's role in this drama. But ultimately she didn't blame him. If anyone was at fault, she was — for believing, for lowering her guard and falling in love again. For making herself vulnerable.

"Everyone says you should marry Sawyer," Susan put in. "If you did, would we still have to leave Hard Luck?"

"If you don't want to marry Sawyer," Scott said, "what about Pete? He's not as good-looking as Sawyer and he's kinda old, but he's real nice, even if he does have his hair in a ponytail. We could live with him, and he's got enough supplies to last us all year."

"I'm not marrying anyone," Abbey said, laughing and crying simultaneously.

"But if you did want to marry

someone, it'd be Sawyer, right?" Scott persisted, his eyes serious. "You really like him. I know you do, because Susan and me saw you kissing, and it looked like you both thought it was fun."

"We're friends," Abbey told her children. "But Sawyer doesn't love me and . . . Oh, I know you're disappointed. I am, too, but we have to move."

Neither of the children said anything.

Abbey sniffed. She wiped her nose with her tissue, then rested her hands on the back of the dining-room chair. The sooner they were gone, she decided, the easier it would be. "Pack everything in your suitcases tonight. We're leaving first thing in the morning with Allison Reynolds."

Sawyer sat alone at the dinner table, his meal untouched. When Charles returned to Hard Luck from one of his jaunts, the two brothers usually sat up and talked most of the night.

Not this time.

In fact, if he saw his older brother just then, Sawyer wouldn't be held accountable for what he said or did.

His own brother had betrayed him by offering to fly Abbey out of Hard Luck. Sawyer had hoped she'd have the sense to realize she belonged right here with him. But apparently not.

Thanks to Charles's interference,

his encouraging Abbey to leave, the two brothers had become involved in a heated argument. They'd parted, furious with each other.

Even now Sawyer couldn't understand how the brother he would've trusted with his life could do this to him. It was obvious that Charles didn't know a thing about falling in love. And even less about women . . .

Sawyer prayed that his older brother would experience — and soon — the intense frustration of loving a woman and being barricaded at every turn. And he *did* love her, damn it.

It was particularly disconcerting when one of those barricades came in the form of his own flesh and blood.

Not for the first time since meeting Abbey, Sawyer appreciated the dilemma his father had been in when his mother had said she wanted a separation. Soon afterward, Ellen had packed her bags and returned to England with Christian.

Sawyer still didn't fully grasp the dynamics of his parents' relationship. He'd known for years that his mother was deeply unhappy. As a child, he'd realized she wasn't like the other women in Hard Luck. She spoke with an accent and tended to keep to herself. As far as Sawyer knew, Pearl Inman had been her only friend. The other women had club meetings and

volunteered at the school, but Ellen was never included.

In some ways she'd been an embarrassment to her son. He'd
wanted her to be like his friends'
mothers. All she ever seemed to
care about were her books — and
yet, ironically, it was those books
that had brought Abbey to Hard
Luck.

Like his father before him, Sawyer
was going to walk down to the
airfield come morning and watch
the woman he loved disappear into
the horizon.

Then, like his father, Sawyer
strongly suspected he was going to
get royally soused, if not falling-
down drunk.

Pushing away his untouched dinner plate, Sawyer stood. He walked into the living room and gazed longingly out the window. Abbey was directly across the street, but she might as well be on the other side of the world.

The urge to breach the distance and tell her everything that was in his heart was like a gnawing hunger that refused to go away. If there was the slightest chance she'd listen to him, he would've done it.

From the corner of his eye, Sawyer saw Scott wheel his old bike toward his house. The boy threw the bike down, then kicked it hard enough to make Sawyer wince.

First the mother and now the boy. Exhaling a deep breath, Sawyer went resolutely to the front door and opened it. He stepped onto the porch. "Is something wrong, son?"

"I'm not your son!" Scott shouted.

"What's wrong?"

Scott kicked the bicycle again. "You can have your dumb old bike. I don't want it. It's stupid and I never liked it."

"Thank you for returning it," Sawyer said without emotion. Scott's display of pain and anger was unlike him. Wondering what — if anything — he should say, Sawyer walked down the steps. "Would you like to help me put it back in the storage shed?"

"No."

Sawyer stooped to pick up the bicycle. The moment he bent to retrieve it, he was attacked with fists and feet. The blows didn't hurt as much as surprise him.

"You made my mother cry!" Scott screamed. "Now we have to leave!"

Sawyer easily deflected the impact of the small fists and wild punches. Scott kicked him for all he was worth, his shoe connecting with Sawyer's shin a number of times.

In an effort to protect himself and Scott, Sawyer dropped the old bike and wrapped his arms around the boy's shoulders. He knelt down on the grass in front of him. By now Scott was crying openly and his breath came in ragged gasps.

Sawyer held him tight, absorbing the boy's pain and feeling as though his own heart was about to break.

Losing Abbey was bad enough. It seemed unfair that he'd lose the children, too.

In the short time they'd lived in Hard Luck, Scott and Susan had captured his heart. A day didn't seem right without Scott there to greet him and ask if he could get Eagle Catcher out of his pen. And Susan . . . With her wide grins and charming enthusiasm, she could always wrap him around her little finger.

"I'm sorry I made your mother cry," Sawyer whispered over and over, although he was sure the boy didn't hear him.

Sobbing, Scott buried his face in Sawyer's shoulder. Soon his thin arms were wrapped around Sawyer's neck and he clung to him as if he'd never let go. "Your bike isn't really stupid," he mumbled.

"I know."

"We have to put everything back in our suitcases," Scott said. "Mom told us at dinner that we're leaving in the morning."

"I know." He didn't bother to hide his regret.

Scott's head jerked back and he stared at Sawyer through swollen eyes. "You do?"

Sawyer nodded.

"And you were just gonna let us leave, without even saying good-bye?"

"I was going to walk down to the field in the morning and see you off," Sawyer explained. *And then silently stand by and watch you fly away.* He had no choice. What else could he do?

"Susan and I don't want to leave."

Sawyer's heart lightened a little. Perhaps Abbey's children could succeed where he'd failed. "Did you tell your mother that?"

Scott's eyes glistened with his recently shed tears. "That made her cry even more. I thought you cared about Mom and Susan and me."

"I do, Scott, more than you'll ever know."

Scott yanked himself free. "Then why does Mom want to move away so bad?"

"Because . . ." Sawyer struggled for words. "Sometimes it isn't easy to understand, especially when you're just nine and —"

"I wouldn't understand it if I live to be as old as . . . as forty."

Sawyer smiled, despite himself. "I wish I understood it myself so I could explain it to you." He stroked the boy's hair. "Do you want to talk about it some more?"

"No," Scott said, and shook his head. Rubbing his eyes with the heel of his hand, he turned and ran in the opposite direction as fast as his legs would carry him.

Sawyer's heart contracted at the boy's distress. He wanted to follow Scott and swear that he'd do anything to convince Abbey to stay in Hard Luck. Anything. Instead, he remained on the front lawn, staring after her son. He hardly noticed that Mitch Harris was walking in his direction.

At Mitch's greeting, he raised a hand and smiled wanly. Presumably the public safety officer wasn't there on official business. In his calm, quiet way, Mitch was the most effective cop they'd ever had, but right now, Sawyer didn't need a cop.

"You certainly look glum," Mitch said, continuing toward him.

Sawyer kept his gaze on the house across the street. "Abbey's leaving," he said flatly.

"You're kidding, I hope. Her daughter and my Chrissie hit it off like gangbusters."

Sawyer nodded.

"It's been great for Chrissie to

have a friend her age," Mitch said, his eyes narrowed in concern. "Those two have been inseparable for the past month. What happened?"

"I can't figure it out." Sawyer massaged his forehead.

"I thought — or rather, I'd heard — that you and Abbey had become . . . good friends."

"I thought we were friends, too. I guess I was wrong. She wants out of Hard Luck."

"Are you going to let her go?"

For pride's sake, Sawyer shrugged as if her coming or going was of little consequence to him. "It seems that bringing women to town was nothing more than an expensive mistake."

"I'm sorry to hear about Abbey and her kids leaving, though," Mitch said. "Chrissie's going to miss Susan, and I suspect Hard Luck's going to miss having a librarian. Abbey would've done a good job if she'd decided to stay. It's a shame."

Sawyer couldn't agree more.

"That's not our only problem," Sawyer said. He went back into the house and brought back a letter addressed to the school board. It was from Margaret Simpson, the high school teacher. "I received this in today's mail," he said and handed it to Mitch.

Mitch quickly scanned the letter. "Margaret's decided not to teach next year, after all."

"That's what she says." She'd addressed the letter to Sawyer as president of the school board. He drew a deep breath. "Looks like we'll need another teacher before the end of the summer. I'll be calling a board meeting later in the week."

"Fine." Mitch paused, then said, "It seems like a lot of bad news all at once, doesn't it?"

Sawyer was staring at the house across the street. "That it does," he murmured.

The two men shook hands, and Mitch left, walking across the street to Abbey's house. Sawyer had never been the nosy type, but he was decidedly curious to learn what Mitch had to say.

Abbey answered the door. Although Sawyer couldn't hear the conversation, he guessed that Mitch was bidding her farewell. But whatever Mitch's business with Abbey, it didn't last long. Hoping he wasn't too obvious, Sawyer tried to sneak a look at her. It didn't work; she was back inside the house faster than a turtle retreating into its shell.

Neither of the children had been particularly cooperative about going to bed. Since the sun still shone brightly at ten o'clock, it was difficult for them to get to sleep. As usual, Abbey propped a board against the curtains to darken the room a little.

She was grateful when the talking

quieted down. Sitting at the kitchen table with her feet on the opposite chair, she sipped from a glass of iced tea and considered her options.

Her suitcases were packed. So were the children's. They'd worked silently, not hiding their disappointment. It was such a contrast, Abbey thought, to their cheerful, excited chatter the night they'd packed to come here.

Before he went to bed, Scott had told her he'd returned Sawyer's bike. Abbey had hugged her son and kissed the top of his head.

Fairbanks wouldn't be so bad, she'd tried to convince herself and the children. It was Alaska's second-largest city, and it would have all the comforts they'd left behind in Seattle.

No reaction.

She'd assured them they'd be settled in and ready long before school started. Even the reminder that Fairbanks was the world's mushing capital didn't seem to raise Scott's spirits. He was going to miss Sawyer's husky.

"Will I ever see Eagle Catcher again?" he'd asked.

"I . . . I don't know," Abbey told him sadly.

Although she knew she wouldn't sleep, she trudged down the hall to her bedroom. Out of habit, she stopped to check on Scott and Susan. Knowing they hadn't been asleep for long, she opened the door a crack and glanced inside.

Both had the covers pulled up over their heads. Quietly she closed the door and slipped down the hall.

She got as far as the second bedroom when she stopped. Something wasn't right. She hesitated, unable to identify exactly what it was. Retracing her steps, she returned to the bedroom, opening the door a bit wider.

Standing where she was, her silhouette against the opposite wall, Abbey could see nothing wrong. Tiptoeing farther into the room, she sat on the edge of Scott's bed.

It was then that she realized it wasn't her son in the bed at all, but a rolled-up blanket and a football helmet.

Abbey gasped, surged to her feet and yanked back the covers.

Scott was missing.

She rushed over to the second bed and discovered that Susan was gone, too.

Abbey turned on the light and saw an envelope leaning against the lamp on the nightstand. She reached for it, her fingers trembling, and tore it open.

Dear Mom,
We don't want to leave Hard Luck. You can go without Susan and me. Don't worry about us.

Love,
Scott and Susan

Abbey read through it four times

before the realization began to sink in. Her children had run away.

She raced to the phone and instinctively dialed Sawyer's number. She felt so shaky she had to punch in the numbers twice.

"Hello."

At least he wasn't asleep. "It's Abbey. Is Eagle Catcher there?"

"You want to talk to my dog?"

"Don't be ridiculous. I want you to check his pen and tell me if he's inside. Please, Sawyer, this is important."

"I can tell you right now that he is," Sawyer grumbled. "I locked him in no more than an hour ago."

"Please check."

He sighed. "Okay."

She heard the click as he set the

428

phone down. Abbey closed her eyes and impatiently counted backward, starting at a hundred, while he left the house to check his backyard. She'd reached sixty-three by the time he got back.

"He's gone," Sawyer said breathlessly. "Abbey, what's going on? Are you okay?"

"No, I'm not okay." Her heart felt like it was about to explode inside her chest. "Scott and Susan are gone."

Without a second's hesitation, Sawyer said, "I'll be right over."

"Please hurry," she whispered, but he'd already severed the connection.

CHAPTER 10

"Where would they go?" Abbey asked even before Sawyer had entered the house. She handed him Scott's letter, which he read in a few seconds.

"I have no idea."

Abbey sank onto the sofa. Her legs were incapable of supporting her any longer. "This is all my fault."

"Blaming yourself isn't going to help find those kids. Think, Abbey! You know Scott and Susan. Where would they hide?"

Abbey buried her face in her hands as she tried to reason, but her mind refused to function. Every time she closed her eyes, all she could see was her two children in the wilderness alone. Sawyer had repeatedly warned them about the dangers lurking out on the tundra. He'd told them about his aunt, who had disappeared without a trace at the age of five. . . .

No one had ever explicitly described the danger brown bears presented, but it was very real. The day after her arrival she'd learned how to operate a can of pepper spray to ward them off. Now her children, the life and breath of her soul, were alone and defenseless, possibly wandering around in the wild. Eagle Catcher could only do so much to protect them.

"I'll find them, Abbey," Sawyer promised. He knelt in front of her and gripped her hands in both of his. "I swear to you I won't stop searching until they're home and safe."

Abbey reached for him. Despite their differences, despite the fact that she was walking out of his life in a few hours, she trusted Sawyer as she did no one else. He'd find her children or die in the attempt. She knew that.

His arms went around her, and they clung to each other.

"Abbey, don't forget — they've obviously got the dog with them.

That's a good thing. Stay here," he instructed her. "I'll alert Mitch and we'll get a search team assembled."

She nodded, well aware that she wouldn't be of any help to them. But she didn't want to be here alone with her fears. Sawyer seemed to realize that, too.

"I'll ask Pearl Inman to come stay with you."

Her heart in her throat, Abbey walked Sawyer to the front door. He raised his hand and gently touched her cheek. Then he was gone.

Abbey moved onto the porch and sat in the swing, nearly choking on her fears. Mosquitoes buzzed nearby, but she paid them no heed. Again and again, her mind went back to the conversation she'd had with the children earlier that evening.

They loved Hard Luck. And Eagle Catcher and Sawyer. Without a bit of trouble, they'd adjusted to their new lives in Alaska. Abbey had assumed it was too soon for any real attachments, but she'd been wrong.

Her son had bonded with Eagle Catcher. He'd become friends with Ronny Gold. Susan had struck up a friendship with Chrissie Harris. And she . . . well, she'd gone and done something really dangerous.

She'd fallen in love with Sawyer O'Halloran. She saw her actions with fresh clarity. Knowing she loved him frightened her so badly she'd decided to run. The fear of making another mistake had caused her to panic.

Pearl appeared on the top porch step. Caught up in her thoughts, Abbey hadn't noticed her right away.

"Abbey?"

"Oh, Pearl," she said in a broken whisper. "I'm so afraid."

The older woman sat next to her and squeezed her shoulders. "Sawyer will find those kids, don't you worry."

"But they could be anywhere."

"Mark my words, they'll be found in short order. At least they were smart enough to take Eagle Catcher. He's a good dog, and he isn't going to let anything happen to them."

Abbey tried to relax, but despite Pearl's assurances, she simply couldn't. The tension wouldn't ease until she knew her children were safe.

"Come on," Pearl said, "let's make a pot of coffee and some sandwiches. The men are going to need them."

Abbey agreed, although she knew Pearl was just trying to get her mind off the children. She moved into the kitchen and began the preparations by rote.

"Are you sure you want to use that much coffee?" Pearl asked, looking up from the bread she was efficiently buttering.

Abbey saw that she'd filled the basket to overflowing. "No," she said, laughing nervously. "Perhaps you'd better make the coffee."

"Sure thing. Just let me finish this."

They sat at the kitchen table and listened to the hot water dripping through the filter. The pot's gurgling seemed strangely loud in the unnatural quiet of the house.

An hour passed, the longest of her life. Mitch stopped by the house and asked Abbey some questions about the kids.

When he left, Pearl poured her a cup of coffee.

"The kids were upset about leaving," Abbey confessed to her.

"You're leaving?" Pearl sounded shocked. "Whatever for?"

"Because . . . oh, I don't know,

because nothing seems right anymore. I'm afraid, Pearl . . . I don't want to be in love. It scares me. And Sawyer . . . I wouldn't have thought it possible to insult a woman with a marriage proposal, but he managed it. He seems to believe that every woman wants to trap him!"

Pearl patted her hand gently. "If that's the case, he must feel very strongly about you, otherwise he'd never have asked."

Despite everything, Abbey smiled. "I think Sawyer's as confused as I am."

When the phone rang, it startled Abbey so much she didn't know what to do. She sat paralyzed, unable to move or even breathe.

Pearl picked up the receiver. "Yes, yes . . ." she said, nodding.

Abbey studied the older woman's face for any sign of news.

A moment later, Pearl held her hand over the mouthpiece. "It's Sawyer. He called to let you know they have two four-man teams searching the area. The first one just reported back. They didn't see any trace of the children. He wants to talk to you."

Abbey snatched the receiver. "Sawyer, what's happening?"

"Nothing yet." How calm and confident he sounded. "Don't worry, we'll find them. Are you all right?"

"No!" she cried. "I want my children!"

"We'll find them, Abbey," he said again. "Don't worry."

She took a deep breath and tried to remain calm. "Is there any sign of Eagle Catcher?" she asked. If they found the dog, then surely the children would be nearby.

"Not yet."

"Call me soon, please. Even if you haven't found them yet. I need to know what's happening."

"I will," he promised.

Pearl poured Abbey another coffee and brought it to her. She stared into it, trying to think.

Another hour dragged slowly by, and Abbey started to pace. This time when the phone rang, she leapt for it.

"Did you find them?" she blurted

into the mouthpiece.

"Mom?"

"Scott, is that you?" Abbey asked, then burst into tears. The release of tension washed over her like . . . like the clear, clean waters of Abbey Lake.

"Don't cry, Mom. We're okay. I bet we're in a lot of trouble. . . . Here, you better talk to Sawyer."

Abbey tried to control her emotions, but the relief was too great to do anything but give in to it. A moment later Sawyer was on the line.

"Abbey, it's me."

"Where were they?"

"We found them in the old lodge. They'd managed to make their way upstairs, where they were hiding. I found the three of them cuddled up together. Eagle Catcher was in the middle and they each had an arm around him."

"You mean to say they were that close to town all this time?"

Sawyer chuckled. "Yup. Eagle Catcher heard me calling him, but he wouldn't leave Scott and Susan."

"Remind me to kiss that dog." She laughed softly.

"I'd rather you kissed the dog's owner."

Abbey's laughter faded, and the tension returned.

"Never mind," Sawyer said, defeated. "It was only a suggestion. The important thing is, the kids are safe and sound. I'll be bringing them home."

"Thank you, Sawyer. Thank you!" She glanced over at Pearl as she replaced the receiver. "They're fine," she said, wiping the tears from her face. "Sawyer found them hiding in the lodge."

"Thank God," Pearl whispered.

"I do," Abbey responded.

"I don't imagine you'll be needing me here anymore." The older woman moved toward the door, then turned toward her. "I know it's none of my affair and I'm sticking my nose where it doesn't belong, but I'd hoped you'd stay on in Hard Luck. You don't need me to tell you how stubborn men can be — and Sawyer's more stubborn than most. But his heart's in the right place."

Uncomfortable with the conversation, Abbey averted her gaze.

"We're gonna miss you and those young'uns," Pearl said sadly, "but you're the one making the decisions."

Abbey walked her to the door, then stood and waited on the porch for Sawyer to deliver her family. He arrived in his truck, along with his brother. When he opened the door, Scott and Susan came charging out of the cab, running straight into Abbey's outstretched arms.

Both children were talking at once, telling their version of what had happened and why. After she'd hugged and kissed them both, she glanced up to see Sawyer standing beside the truck, watching them. Charles was inside the cab.

"It seems to me you've caused a lot of trouble," she told the children. "You'll both be writing letters of apology to each and every person who searched for you."

Scott hung his head and nodded. Susan did, too.

"I'm sorry, Mom," Scott said, "but we don't want to move to Fairbanks. We like it here."

"We'll discuss this in the morning. We'll also discuss your punishment, and it's going to be more than just writing the letters. Understand?"

They nodded again.

"Now go and take a bath, both of you — you're absolutely filthy.

445

Then get back into bed. We have a busy day ahead of us."

"But, Mom —"

"Good night, Scott. Good night, Susan," she said pointedly.

Their heads hanging, the two youngsters went inside the house.

Abbey looked at Sawyer. Swallowing hard, she approached him. "Sawyer, I don't have the words to thank you properly," she said, wrapping her arms around her waist. She smiled hesitantly at him. Even now, the temptation to walk into his arms tempted her almost beyond endurance. It struck her as deeply significant that when she'd discovered her children were missing, he was the person she'd turned to.

"I'm glad they're safe," Sawyer said. "That's what matters."

They stared at each other, neither of them saying a word or moving a step closer.

An eternity seemed to pass before Charles stuck his head out the cab window and cleared his throat. "We'll be seeing you in the morning, right?"

Abbey glanced from Sawyer to Charles. "In the morning," she said, then turned and walked away.

"You look like you could use a good, stiff drink," Charles said when Sawyer climbed back into the truck.

Sawyer's eyes were fixed on the front door of the house. It'd take a lot more than whiskey to cure what ailed him.

"I'll drive you back to your place," he said impassively. His hands tightened around the steering wheel until the knuckles showed white.

"You're in love with her." Charles's voice was matter-of-fact.

"Is that so hard to believe?"

"You barely know the woman!"

Hot anger surged through Sawyer. "I know what I feel. I know that when Abbey and those two kids board the plane you're piloting tomorrow, they're taking a part of me with them."

"You're serious?"

"Yes, I'm serious!" Sawyer snapped.

Charles didn't say anything until

his brother pulled up in front of his house, which was at the other end of town near the lodge. "I was wrong to get involved."

It was of absolutely no comfort to hear Charles admit it now.

"I sure don't think this scheme of yours and Christian's was one of your brighter moves, but you obviously care for Abbey and those children."

His brother wouldn't understand how much he did care until he'd fallen in love himself. "That's putting it mildly."

"So, are you going to let her leave?"

"What choice do I have?" Sawyer asked, frustration ringing in his voice. How many people were going to ask him this? "I can't hold her hostage. I've tried talking to her, and that doesn't do any good. Mainly because every time I open my mouth to tell her how I feel, I end up insulting her. I get all tongue-tied and stupid."

Charles seemed to find Sawyer's confession amusing. He smiled.

"I've never . . . felt this way before," Sawyer said in his own defense, "and I'm telling you right now, watch out, because it's like getting hit with the worse case of flu you've ever had. Your turn's coming, so get that smug smile off your face."

"No way," Charles insisted. "I don't want any part of it. Look what it's done to you."

"You think I wanted this? It just *happened*. Abbey arrived — and there I was with my tongue hanging out."

Charles laughed outright. "How is it, little brother, that we've lived to the ripe old ages of thirty-three and thirty-five without falling in love?"

"And we were proud of it, weren't we, big brother?" Now it was Sawyer's turn to be amused. "Not anymore. When I met Abbey, I felt like I'd been sucker-punched. So I did everything I could to get rid of her."

"What made her finally decide to leave?"

"You mean other than my marriage proposal?"

Charles laughed. "So you scared her into it."

"I was serious," he said with a sigh. "All right, maybe I didn't use fancy words and tell her the angels smiled on her the day she was born and drivel like that, but I meant what I said." He paused as the regret sank in. "Maybe I could've been a bit more romantic, though."

"What'd you say to her?"

"Well —" Sawyer thought back to their conversation "— I don't exactly remember. We were at Ben's and there were a lot of people around, so I sort of stood next to her and said I didn't think it was a good idea for her to marry Pete or any of the other men who'd proposed."

"You mean to say she had more than one offer?"

"Yes." Sawyer's fingers threatened to dent the steering wheel. "Besides Pete, I think Ralph might've asked her, too."

"So you stood next to her at Ben's . . ."

"Right. We were welcoming Allison Reynolds, and basically I told Abbey that if she was so keen to get married she should've spoken up earlier because I was willing to marry her."

Charles was quiet for a long time. "That's it?" he eventually said.

Sawyer nodded.

"You didn't ask for my advice, but I'll give it to you, anyway. If I were you I'd propose again, and this time I'd use a few of those fancy words you frown on."

"I don't know if I can," Sawyer said sadly.

"Can you live with the alternative?" Charles asked.

"I don't know," he said. "I just don't know."

After dropping his brother off, Sawyer returned to his own place. He checked on Eagle Catcher, talking to the dog for a few minutes, then walked into the house. It felt empty and silent. He fixed a drink and took it into his bedroom, where he spent some time studying the photographs of his parents that stood on the dresser.

Tugging his shirttail free, he undressed and readied for bed. It was going to be a long night. Lying on his back, hands behind his head, he stared at the ceiling and tried to work out his options.

What he'd told his brother was true. When Abbey left Hard Luck she'd be taking part of him with her. He had to prove that to her. He just didn't know how.

He wasn't a man of words. He'd demonstrated that repeatedly; he'd made a mess of things whenever he opened his mouth. But there *had* to be a way to show Abbey he loved her.

He hardly slept at all.

By six he was up and dressed again. He sat at the kitchen table, nursing his coffee, devising a plan.

He waited until eight, then gathered together what he needed. He walked purposefully across the street to Abbey's.

He hadn't even reached the front door when she opened it. She wore a pretty pink sweater and jeans, and she'd never looked more beautiful.

"Good morning," she said. He noticed how pale she was. Pale and miserable. As miserable as he felt.

"Morning."

"I know you're busy getting ready to leave, so I won't take any more of your time than necessary. I brought something over for Scott and Susan," he said. "And you."

"The children are still sleeping."

"It doesn't matter. I'll give everything to you, and you can see that they get it later."

"Sawyer, I've been thinking and really there isn't any need —"

"Would it be all right if we sat down?" He motioned toward the swing.

Abbey sighed and perched on the swing's edge. Sawyer had the impression she'd rather avoid this last encounter. He didn't blame her.

They sat on opposite sides, as if they were uncomfortable strangers. He handed her an envelope. "These are Eagle Catcher's registration papers. I'm giving him to Scott — it'll make the transition easier. Once you're settled, let me know and I'll have him delivered."

"But he's *your* dog."

Sawyer's smile was sad. He

wouldn't tell her that relinquishing the husky was more difficult than she'd ever know. "Those two belong together."

"But Sawyer —"

"Please, Abbey, let me do this one thing."

She looked as though she wanted to argue, then bit her lower lip and nodded.

"Susan is a wonderful little girl," Sawyer said. "I thought long and hard about what I could give her." He reached inside his shirt pocket and withdrew a gold, heart-shaped pendant. "This is a locket that belonged to my grandmother." He opened the tiny clasp with difficulty. "The picture inside is of Emily, the daughter she lost. She gave it to me shortly before she died. I'd like you to keep it until Susan's old enough to wear it."

Tears welled in Abbey's eyes as he placed the locket and its delicate chain in the palm of her hand. "Sawyer, I . . . I don't know what to say."

Sawyer's heart was heavy. "I have no other way of showing you how much I love you and Scott and Susan." He stood and took out an envelope from his pants pocket. It contained two marbles, a bobby pin and several folded sheets of paper. He sat down, then retrieved a second envelope from his shirt pocket.

"The last things I have are for you." He gave her the bobby pin first. "This saved my life when I was sixteen. It's a long, complicated story that I won't go into, but I was flying alone in the dead of winter and I had engine trouble. Had to make an emergency landing. This bobby pin was on the floor of the plane, and it helped me fix the problem so I could get back in the air and home. Otherwise I would've frozen to death. I saved the pin." He set it carefully aside.

Abbey smiled.

"The marbles were my two favorites as a kid. I was better than anyone, and these were the prize of my collection. Mom ordered them for me from a Sears catalog."

Abbey held the two marbles in her free hand.

He passed her the folded sheets

of paper. "These are old and a bit yellowed, but you should still be able to read them. The first is an essay I wrote when I was in junior high. I won a writing contest with it and got a letter of commendation from the governor. His letter's with the story."

Abbey used the back of her hand to wipe the tears from her face.

Sawyer withdrew a plain gold band from the second envelope. "This is my father's wedding ring." Sawyer held it up between two fingers. His heart seized with pride and pain at the sight of it. "Since I was the one with Dad when he died, Charles and Christian thought I should have it. It's probably not worth much, but I treasure it." He leaned forward to place the ring in Abbey's hand and closed her fingers over it. Afraid he might have said more than he should, he stood up and awkwardly shoved his hands in his pockets. "Goodbye, Abbey."

As he turned to leave, she called to him. "Sawyer."

He faced her.

"Why are you giving me these things?"

"The bobby pin and marbles and the essay and Dad's ring — they represent what I am. I can't go with you and I can't make you stay, so I'm giving you part of me to take when you leave."

He was halfway down the steps when he heard her whisper. "You might have said you loved me earlier."

He kept his back to her and answered. "I want to marry you. A man doesn't propose to a woman unless he loves her."

"He does if he's afraid some other man might beat him to the punch. He does if he's confused about what he really wants."

"I know what I want," Sawyer said, turning, and his eyes met hers.

"Do you, Sawyer?"

"I want to spend the rest of my life with you, right here in Hard Luck. I want to raise Scott and Susan as my own children, and if you and God are willing, I'd like another child or two."

They stood staring at each other,

the depth of their emotion visible. Abbey's beautiful brown eyes glistened with tears. It demanded every bit of self-control Sawyer possessed not to bridge the distance between them and take her in his arms.

"But I can't have that," he said, "so I'm giving you the most valuable things I own to do with as you please." Having said that, he hurried down the remaining steps.

"If you walk away from me now, Sawyer O'Halloran, I swear I'll never forgive you."

He turned around again to find her standing on the top step, her arms open. The sweetest smile he'd ever seen lit her eyes, curved her mouth.

His heart came to a sudden standstill. Then he rushed back, throwing his arms around her waist, pulling her tight against him. He trembled with the shock of it. He kissed her gently at first, for fear of frightening her with the power of his need.

Abbey slipped her arms around his neck and moaned. A stronger, more disciplined man might have been able to resist her, but not Sawyer. Not when he feared he'd never hold her and kiss her again. Not when he'd laid his heart and his life at her feet.

They kissed once more, too hungry for each other to attempt restraint. It was as if all the barriers had disappeared.

When he could, Sawyer pulled his

mouth from hers, inhaled deeply and buried his face in her neck. He prayed for the strength to stop; otherwise, he was afraid he'd end up making love to her right then and there. But Abbey drew his face to hers, and the kissing began all over again.

"I think you should marry me," he breathed between kisses.

"A woman prefers to be asked, Sawyer O'Halloran."

"Please, Abbey, if you have any feelings for me whatsoever, put me out of this misery and marry me."

"Are you asking me or telling me?"

"Begging."

He felt the rush of air from Abbey's laugh before she kissed him.

A kiss that was deep, passionate, thorough.

"Is that your answer?" he panted when she'd finished.

"Yes. But first you need to understand something. I'm not very good at this wife thing. I've got one failure behind me, and . . . Oh, Sawyer, I'm scared."

"Of what? Making another mistake?"

"No, not that. Not with you. I'm afraid . . . of so many things. Dick had several affairs, and when we divorced, he said . . . he said I'd never make a man happy."

"You make me happy. Did I ever tell you how much I love it when you smile?"

Abbey blushed. "I don't mean it

like that. I don't know if I'll . . . satisfy you."

Sawyer threw back his head and laughed. "Oh, Abbey, just holding you gives me so much pleasure I can't even begin to imagine what it's going to be like in bed."

Sawyer could see that she was about to argue with him, so he guided her mouth to his and kissed her with all the love in his heart. He tasted her hesitation and her anxiety, then felt her yield to his kiss.

For the first time Sawyer understood the root of Abbey's fears. "You satisfy me," he whispered. "And tantalize me and torment me."

"Mom?"

Sawyer looked past Abbey to see Scott and Susan in the doorway. They were both still in their pajamas, their faces eager and wide-awake.

"Good morning," Sawyer said. "I've got some great news for you."

"You do?" Susan asked.

"Your mother's agreed to marry me."

Scott seemed mildly puzzled. "Already? Mom, I thought you said it would take a while to work everything out. The problems between you and Sawyer, I mean."

"Work out our problems?" Sawyer was the one wearing the perplexed frown this time.

"The children and I talked after you found them last night," Abbey explained. "We decided it would be a mistake to leave Hard Luck. Furthermore, we decided we're in love with you."

"You mean you weren't going to leave this morning?"

Abbey's arms tightened around him. "Don't sound so disappointed."

"I'm not. It's just that . . ." He stiffened. "You might have told me."

"I tried, but you wouldn't let me. Are you sorry about . . . what you said? The things you gave me?"

"No," he said fervently. "Not in the least."

"Are you really going to marry us?" Susan wanted to know.

"Yup."

"When?" This was from Scott, who continued to look unsure.

Sawyer and Abbey exchanged a glance. "Two weeks," Sawyer said, making the decision for them.

"Two weeks!" Abbey cried.

"I've been waiting thirty-three years for you, Abbey Sutherland, and I refuse to wait a minute longer than I have to. We'll do this as plain or as fancy as you want. Ben can cater the wedding, and we'll open up the school gym for the reception."

A truck pulled up in front of the house and the driver honked. "Looks like you two have everything settled," Charles called, leaning his elbow out the window.

"Sure do."

"Guess you won't be needing me, then."

"Sawyer's going to marry Mom and us," Susan informed him with her wide, delightful grin.

"In two weeks," Scott added.

"So you're not letting any grass grow under your feet," Charles commented.

"Nope," Sawyer said.

"Is this a secret or can I spread the word?" Charles asked.

Abbey and Sawyer looked at each other and smiled. "Feel free," Sawyer told him.

Charles pounded the horn and stuck his head out the window as he drove down the street, shouting, "There's going to be a wedding in Hard Luck!"

"You can't change your mind now, Sawyer."

"No chance of that," he whispered. "No chance at all."